An Extra Curvy Love

MELVINA CARPENTER

Dedication...

This book is dedicated to every woman who needs to be reminded of your beauty, strength, and charisma, regardless of your color, height or weight. There's someone out there who will love every inch of you!

ACKNOWLEDGMENTS

Thank you so much for your support and purchase of one or more of my books. I hope that you enjoyed it! Please remember to write a review and tell others about me as well.

EXCERPT…

"I meant to tell you that my daughters will be here this weekend. I'd love for you to meet them."

"Your-your daughters?" Zoe stuttered.

"Yes!" He took both of Zoe's hands into his and looked into her eyes. "I believe the prophet, Zoe. I also believe that I've personally heard God concerning you. I want you to meet my daughters. I don't want to waste any time with you. Are you ok with that?"

"Umm, yes, I think so. I'm just nervous."

"For what? They're going to love you!" He planted one more kiss on her cheek and opened his car door to leave. Her lips were a bit swollen from him kissing her earlier. He came to her once more and stole another kiss. Without realizing it, he'd pinned her to his vehicle while he kissed her. He lost all sense of consciousness as his lower body moved against her on its own accord. Zoe felt way more than she expected and began to push him away. Thad only tightened his grip.

Table of Contents

Chapter 1

An Interstate Blues

Trying to put on a waist trainer at six-thirty in the morning was harder than doing five pushups for Zoe. Who wears a waist trainer in the middle of July anyway? That's just ludicrous. It's like ninety-two degrees and the sun's not even fully out yet! It would've been easier to just purchase clothing that fit better, but Zoe had to work with what she had.

The work day hadn't even begun yet and she Zoe was already tired. Thank God, she had no children or husband yet! Imagining kissing and sending them off to school and work was a daily daydream and a nightly torture.

Now, at the age of thirty-nine, single and with no prospects, Zoe was feeling exhausted all the time. She was exhausted due to the mental strain of being alone and pretending to be ok. However, the fact of the matter was that she was far from ok. She felt that at any moment, her wall could come tumbling down. Behind that wall would be the real person. Behind that wall would be the woman who hid her true being from the world. The person behind that wall cried herself to sleep at night and dreaded seeing her sized sixteen-eighteen figure in the mirror every morning. Behind that wall, stands a slouching woman who applies more makeup than necessary to hide the pain that seems to creep into every line in her face.

Although she was only thirty-nine, she felt fifty-nine! She was tired of mentally and spiritually fighting the demons in her head that came to torture her daily. She felt worn out. She wanted to give up!

With the waist trainer finally on, clothes smoothed, and makeup applied, Zoe was ready to face the world. Quickly, she grabbed her ready-made chicken salad and cooler mist flavored Gatorade from the fridge. She scurried to set her house alarm and headed for her car.

Her 2014 Toyota corolla wasn't much to many, but it was the world to her. It was paid for! She paid it off fifteen months earlier than scheduled. She prided herself on having the least amount of debt as possible.

She started her vehicle and left her home in Summerville, South Carolina to head to work. She sighed in frustration with the foreknowledge of the heavy traffic. What should've taken her fifteen minutes to get to work extended to almost an hour some days because of the traffic. Mali Music's "Yahweh" blasted through her blue-tooth while she tapped her manicured fingernails on the steering wheel and moved her head to the beat.

"This is some 'get ya going' music for sure," she said to herself. Her excitement ended quickly though.

Now at a standstill on interstate 26, with nothing but brake lights in view, aggravation really set in!

She silently prayed. "Lord, how much longer? How long will my life be like this? How long Lord, before I get to share in the joys of marriage and parenthood? I want to travel, go out and enjoy my life. My family and friends are great but Lord, I need a husband."

She leaned her head against the headrest and felt a tear run down her neck. It startled her because she didn't even realize that she had been crying. Just then, she heard the sound of a car horn and began to lift her foot off the brakes to proceed and almost hit the car in front of her. Her heart was beating unbelievably fast. She frantically looked around to see who blew the horn. It was someone who was driving a beat up, navy blue Honda Accord. The car looked as if it had been in one too many accidents!

To her left, she noticed a gentleman in a very nice black car. He looked to be between the age of forty-eight to fifty years old. He had a darker complexion compared to Zoe's hazelnut colored skin. He was almost the color of a dark chocolate Hershey candy bar. She unconsciously licked her lips at the thought of him. He had salt and pepper hair, full pouty lips, thick eyebrows, and the most perfect nose. She turned her radio down because it was as if she couldn't hear and see at the same time.

Whatever he was listening to or thinking about caused him to smile and her heart leaped at the sight of it! Not only did her heart leap but her insides melted in ways that she hadn't experienced in years.

She was staring at him but didn't even realize what she was doing. This man had captured her attention. The person in the beat-up Honda blew their horn again. However, this time, they held it and waved obscenities to tell her to go. She was sitting still and the cars in front of her had left. The gentleman, the mystery man, drove alongside of her watching her with a look of concern. She suddenly became extremely nervous. She didn't understand why. She then began to quiz herself.

"Why are you nervous, Zoe? He's just a guy! A very attractive guy, but just a guy none-the-less. Get a hold of yourself chick!"

She tried to focus on the road, but she looked his way again and he waved but had a look on his face that wasn't quite friendly. She couldn't make out what he might be thinking. Perhaps he was aggravated that she was watching him and holding up traffic. When she proceeded along, he moved behind her. She could feel her heart thumping through her chest.

"Who is this guy and why is he following ME? Is he following me? Maybe we're both headed in the same direction," she mumbled to herself. "Ugh!" She yelled and slammed her hand on the steering wheel in frustration. "Maybe I should stop talking to myself. He probably thinks I'm crazy!"

Zoe approached her exit. She had never been happier to see the East Montague exit before in her life. She glanced into the rear-view mirror and saw him.

"Wait, why is he still behind me?" She whispered in a whining voice.

She quickly peaked in the mirror above her steering wheel and realized that she'd cried a lot more than she knew. In a panic, she quickly reached for the near empty box of Kleenex from her center console and dabbed her eyes. Her eyeliner smudged a little and the tracks of her tears showed through her foundation. She parked her car and dug through her purse for her cosmetic bag. She couldn't go into work looking like this. She had to keep up the 'all is well' appearance. She found her cosmetic bag but just as she unzipped it, she saw the shadow of someone nearing her vehicle.

"Oh no!" Zoe panicked.

Just that quick she'd forgotten all about the stranger who had been following her. Although she was briefly intrigued by this man, her appearance superseded the thought of him. Zoe took much pride in what she looked like. Her make-up, hair, clothes, nails, everything, had to be just right. Just because she was plus sized didn't mean she wasn't or couldn't be a head turner.

In fact, she turned many heads, she just needed to be more confident to see what they saw.

Mr. Just a Guy lightly tapped on her front driver side window.

Hesitantly, she lowered the window and said, "Yes, may I help you?" She sounded aggravated and nervous at the same time.

He caught onto her tone and quickly held his hands up, while taking a step back as a sign of not wanting any trouble.

"Good morning," he quickly said. "I'm not here to bother or harass you but you looked pretty upset on the interstate."

Her eyes softened, and he leaned in towards her window a little more, so she could hear him over the cars passing by.

"I'm a Pastor and I felt led to check on you. Are you ok? Is there anything I can do to help you?" He reached into his pocket and pulled out a white handkerchief and passed it to her. She realized that he noticed the tear stains on her face because she hadn't touched up her make-up yet.

Reluctantly, she took the handkerchief and thanked him. She had no choice because she forgot to restock on Kleenex for her car. The handkerchief carried a scent that was practically hypnotizing. Immediately the nervousness went away, and Zoe was almost back to herself.

"Thank you, but no thank you, Pastor. I appreciate you checking on me, but I'm alright." She reached for the power button to put her window up again.

"Wait," he said, smiling. He had startled her a bit. "Here's my card. If you're ever looking for a church home, please stop by and visit us. The service times are listed on the card. I honestly meant no harm, but if you were my mom or my sister, I would appreciate someone caring for them as much."

She slowly reached for the card. and looked at it but didn't pay attention to what it said. She glanced back up at him and saw the sincerity in his eyes.

"Thank you," she said shyly.

He patted the hood of her car and said, "Good day to you ma'am," he then walked away.

Zoe caught another glimpse of him through her side view mirror as she rolled her window back up. Her finger seemed to be paralyzed. She was entranced by his every move. His stride was one of mere perfection. He was smooth! He walked with a confidence that was breathtaking. He walked like a man with somewhere to go. His walk seemed to part the Red Sea among other things! He was well dressed and cladded in some very nice attire. He wore brown pointed toe shoes designed, by Jason of Beverly Hills, with a pair of khaki colored slacks that were professionally creased. His shirt was long-sleeved and freshly pressed with a brown stripe around the bottom of the collar. It was obviously an Yves Saint Laurent original. His cuffs were held in place with a brown and gold Trinity De Cartier cufflink with the initial 'W' on it. His scent made her want to do very inappropriate things to him! It was even on the card that he gave her. It was like an oil of some sort and it lingered when he walked away.

She heard him start his car, a very nice, well-shined, black, Maybach 57. She could see from her side-view mirror that it had chrome wheels, leather seats and a license plate that read "Pastor" on the front of the car.

"Dang! His car almost cost more than my entire house," she said out loud to herself! "I've got to stop talking to myself and crying in my car! I don't need any more preachers following me and telling me what they feel in their spirit."

She started plundering through her cosmetic bag again, when she heard a voice through her partially lowered window. She never put it up because she was too busy watching him.

"Girl, what are you doing sitting in this car talking to yourself?"

It was her best friend, Tyler. She and Tyler had become friends when she started cosmetology school. Now, they both owned and worked at the Love, Grace and Peace hair salon. She looked up and giggled a little at the expression on Tyler's face and motherly stance with her hand on her hip.

"Chile, you look like your puppy pooped on your brand new $3000 sofa, had diarrhea when he did it, and then ran away!"

Zoe placed her hands and head on the steering wheel, shook her head and laughed a little harder at her friend. She then sat up and said, "Let me fix my makeup and then I'll come inside and tell you all about it."

"Ok girl, I'll see you inside then." Tyler marched her way into the hair salon while Zoe touched up her face. The last thing she needed was for the women in the hair salon to think that anything was wrong in her life.

Zoe exited her vehicle, grabbed her purse, her carry bag and proceeded to enter the salon. They had five other stylists that worked in the salon as well. The salon's location was perfect being that it was right across from the Tanger Outlet. It's orange color, with stucco siding, made it hard to miss. Zoe and Tyler didn't have to work if they didn't want to. The stylists were paid hourly and the profits were divided between salon expenses and then the owners. The doors were constantly opening and closing with clients coming in and out. They're clients loved the ambiance of the salon and so did they. It was decorated with mahogany hard wood floors and mustard colored walls. The stylist stations were black with a hint of bling on the mirrors and aligned with the most comfortable styling chairs in town. The drying station was no longer a strenuous task for the clients either. The chairs were actually massage chairs, with an elevation feature for the feet. So, while the client's hair dried, their backs were massaged too! Word of mouth traveled quickly and within a year, Zoe and Tyler had more clients than they could handle. They immediately hired other stylist to come and work for them.

The seven of them became a family. However, Zoe and Tyler had a bond that was beyond the other five stylists. They had more in common, they both were praise and worship leaders, preached, were raised in church and focused on things that the others probably thought were boring.

As soon as Zoe locked up her purse and set her carry bag down, Tyler was on her heels.

"So, what's up? Why are you smiling for no reason at all," Tyler asked?

Zoe shook her head at Tyler and went to turn on some jazz to lighten the mood in the salon. She proceeded with folding towels from the night before that were left undone.

"I met someone this morning that was F-I-N-E!" She said this in the most exaggerated, and breathy tone that she could muster. "Girl, he looked good, smelled good and was well-dressed. He even drove a nice car too! You know I'm not superficial or anything, but it was hard not to notice!"

"Wow! Well don't hold back. Tell me how you met. What's his name? What does he do? Are you two going out?" Tyler spewed all the questions out in one breath.

"Unfortunately, we met because I was on the interstate being emotional and he followed me here out of concern."

"He did not!" Tyler said in shock.

"Umm, yeah, he did actually. I was so embarrassed. It turns out that he's a Pastor though. He's older and very distinguished looking. He's very attractive but he wasn't flirting Tyler. He was just checking on me like a good ole' rev would do," she said while smirking.

"Well, what's his name?" Tyler quizzed further.

"I don't know. He gave me a card, but I threw it in my bag."

"Alright. I understand but why were you being emotional though? It must've been pretty bad for him to follow you here!"

Zoe chuckled a little. "Girl, I was on the interstate praying and crying so much that I had people tooting their horns at me. He noticed and followed me to make sure I was ok. There's no more to the story. I promise. I was just feeling some type of way. Trying to pull this girdle up this morning over these size sixteen-eighteen but sometimes eighteen-twenty curves had me in my feelings. I guess it affected me more than it should've."

Tyler listened empathetically because she already knew where this was going. They were both plus sized women, but it didn't bother Tyler as much. Tyler had three children at home and a wonderful husband to embrace her every night. That wasn't Zoe's story. She only had Mr. Hundley, her 8lb Yorkie. He was her companion. He sat with her when she was at home and accompanied her wherever she was permitted to take him. She sometimes even brought him to work with her. The clients loved Mr. Hundley and he loved them right back!

"I understand, Zoe. You know I haven't been a size two in a long time either! Hey, this is off topic, but I meant to ask you if you were free to do praise and worship for me tonight? Our Pastor has to preach at another church downtown and I'm a little hoarse. I can sing backup, but I can't lead."

"Oh, no ma'am! Mr. Hundley and I will be cuddled on my couch watching Hallmark movies tonight. I'm not going anywhere once I leave this salon. Sorry, boo!"

"Man, stop playing. I need your help for real. I'll treat you to lunch on Saturday to wherever you choose. Please, Zoe! I really do need your help!"

"Alright, alright. I'll be there. What time does it start?

"Be there at 7:30pm sharp!"

"Ok. I'll be there. You better be glad that I like you a little bit."

"Thank you so much!" Tyler jumped up and hugged Zoe's shoulders, but Zoe didn't hug her back. Instead, she rolled her eyes.

Tyler laughed. "Whatever, you know you love me!"

Just then some of the other stylist began strolling into the salon. So did Zoe's first client for the day. She would be receiving a shampoo, deep condition and twist out hair style. Zoe loved working on natural hair due to the fact that she was also a naturalist. She loved the afro-centric look that she displayed. Zoe draped her client and led her to the shampoo bowl.

Chapter 2

Preparation for What...

Zoe had a full day at the salon. She prided herself on giving each client the time and service that they needed. She never overbooked so each client had her all to themselves. After her first client, she had three others come in. One to have a crochet done with faux locs, the other a shampoo and set with cornrows to wear beneath her wig, and the last client wanted a bantu knots style. Her wrists, back, calves, ankles, and feet were hurting by the time she was done. Nevertheless, she had to continue with part two of her day.

After cleaning and closing the salon, she headed home to prepare for church. Once again traffic was heavy but not nearly as bad as what she experienced during her morning commute. She sighed with relief when she pulled into the driveway of her home.

She leaned her head against the headrest and inwardly thanked the Lord for the home he blessed her with. She lived in a four-bedroom, two-story home with a loft in a very prominent part of town. She loved the fact that she also had a garage with no windows because she didn't want anyone to be able to see if she was home. Her family members were known for coming over unannounced and she was known for not answering the door. That garage door came in handy especially on the days when she just wanted to hide out. It was also guaranteed privacy if she had a guest over.

She loved her life, but loneliness beat her up sometimes. Especially now that the seasons were changing. The Fourth of July had just ended, and it was time for couples to cuddle a little more on the couch. Although it was still warm outside, it was beginning to get darker earlier. It was during these times that she loved late appointments. It kept her mind occupied and her body out of trouble! She always felt more pressed to have a husband or pray more for a husband around this time of year. The holidays were soon approaching and the church people were horrible to be around. They always wanted to know when she was getting married or when she would bring a man to church or church functions. It frustrated her, yet she always kept her cool. If they only knew how many nights she cried, they would think before they spoke. She thought of all the holiday banquets, marriages, and proms she assisted with by doing the ladies hair and make-up. She then had to show up to the banquets, fully dressed only to serve the married couple's dinner. It almost felt as if she was being punished for not being married. Just then, a jogger with a black and white Great Dane dog caught her attention in her rear-view mirror and quickly pulled her away from her thoughts. She pressed the garage door opener, gathered her things and went into her home.

Mr. Hundley was barking as soon as she turned her key into the washroom door as she exited the garage. She emerged into the kitchen and there he was, jumping up and down with joy because he missed her so much. She missed him even more! She put her purse down and hung her key on the key rack. He was already standing on his hind legs with his front paws leaning on her while he waited to be picked up. She giggled, scooped him up and gave him the hug and baby-like rock that he craved. He tried to give her kisses by licking her face, but she hated that. She moved her face out of his reach, hugged him once more and sat him down on the floor. His long black and brown hair danced on the floor around him as he barked and ran in circles with excitement. She mentally thanked God that he didn't shed, or she wouldn't be able to keep him with all of that hair.

"Alright Mr. Hundley, Mommy's got to get ready for church! Duty calls once again."

Zoe walked into the living room and around the corner past the front door to go upstairs. Mr. Hundley was right on her heels. As soon as she reached the upstairs she smiled at the ambiance of her loft. She was proud of herself because she purchased this home without a cosigner and needed little to no down payment. She maintained her credit to live in this type of home.

She kicked off her black crocs and dug her toes into the carpet. Her loft was child-friendly but romantic at the same time. She had a wrap-around gray leather sofa with gray rustic coffee tables. Silver lamps adorned the coffee tables with yellow lampshades. A midsized yellow bookshelf sat in a corner with children's books and a few board games. A forty-inch flat screen tv mounted the wall with the remote too high for sticky little fingers to reach. She had several nieces and nephews. Whenever she hosted gatherings, this is where the children would hang out at. She peeked into the other two bedrooms and admired how neat they were. They were dressed in neutral colors for whomever visited. A full bathroom sat on the opposite end of the bedrooms. It too was in yellow and silver. Paintings hung on the walls in sporadic places throughout the upstairs. She placed her office downstairs near the kitchen. She didn't want anything work related to be in the area where sleep and relaxation were to take place.

With a relaxed moan, Zoe went into her bedroom and looked into the closet. She pulled out three outfits that she could wear without having to 'work' to put them on. She didn't like any of them. She finally decided on a black, high waisted knee-length, bodycon dress with a huge bow in the front near the left shoulder. The dress had an asymmetrical ruffle layer covering the waistline. She pulled out a pair of zig zag fishnet stockings and some simple black stilettos to wear along with it. This dress did not need jewelry to accessorize it. Her curves did a better job than any piece of jewelry ever could. However, she decided to wear a simple silver Michael Kors watch. Pleased with her selection, she went into her master bathroom and prepared to take a quick but hot shower. It was now six-fifteen and she was pressed for time. After emerging from the shower, she covered her body in a coconut mint body butter with matching body spray then got dressed. She pinned her untwisted hair up into a half mohawk. Even within its curly state, the back hung a little past her shoulders and the front had to be side swept around her right eye because of its length. She applied her makeup and stamped it with corvette red colored lipstick. She felt better about how she looked. Her emotions regarding her weight were on a seesaw. She was up on some days and down on others. Tonight, she was definitely on the up!

She filled her black Michael Kors bag with her essentials for church, grabbed her iPad with the bible app already on it and headed downstairs. She took hold of her keys, set the alarm and proceeded to leave. Mr. Hundley went to his feeding bowl just as she was leaving. It was set on a timer to dispense food, and water. He used his doggy door to go outside for the bathroom and was trained to come right back in. She smiled at him, shut the door and got into her car. She backed out the driveway, pressed the button to close her garage and headed to church. It was now seven o' clock and she was cruising with not a care in the world. Although she was tired, she had energy when it came to God. She loved God and his people. She had her 'Lord, when will it be my turn' moments but she honestly lived to please Him.

Needless to say, she wasn't perfect. She'd been in a couple of relationships and had fallen into temptation more times than she'd like to remember. Nevertheless, she always got back up. She wasn't like some of the women that she knew in church. She didn't sleep with just anyone. If she did sleep with someone, they were in a relationship. It didn't make it right, but you get the picture. She turned over a new leaf. She was determined to wait until marriage. It wasn't easy though. She loved the Lord, but she loved sex too. The Single's group in her church only frustrated her because they acted as if they never had desires or as if that part of their body was numb. Well hers certainly wasn't! She just put a mandate on herself to fast and pray more. She also did a better job of not putting herself in situations where fornicating was easy. Lately, she needed some intercession because her body was on fire! She wanted to remain blessed therefore, she remained celibate, no matter what it took!

She arrived at the address Tyler gave her at the salon. The name of the church, *Life in The Word Modern Ministries*, was in lights. The parking lot attendants were very friendly, not to mention, handsome. Some wore wedding rings, and some didn't. Zoe never went to church to look for a husband but what better place for him to find her?

Tyler was waiting in the foyer of the church when she saw Zoe approaching, her mouth dropped open in astonishment. "Girl, where are you going, to a photo shoot or something? You look absolutely stunning my Sista!"

Zoe blushed and giggled. "Girl...Tyler, you're a mess! Let's go over these songs before service starts. We only have ten minutes to get it together."

"Ok, well I was thinking that I could lead, *Jehovah, You I Trust,* and you could lead, *Hallelujah, You've Won the Victory*," Tyler chimed in.

"Alright, sounds good to me but you know I'm all about going with the flow," Zoe warned.

"Yeah, yeah, I know," Tyler said. She was still feeling tired from having to get up so early to dress her three children and lay her husband's clothing out for church. She was a true domestic woman. She even cooked dinner for them before she left. They were all seated inside in support of their Pastor and of course Tyler.

Tyler and Zoe sat on the front row. A person from the sound department came and placed microphones in their hands for them to test. Everything was good. Zoe bowed her head and closed her eyes and the musician played something unfamiliar but worship provoking in the background. She was startled when she heard a voice in the microphone near the front of the church. She looked up and her voice got caught in her throat. She grabbed Tyler's wrist and slowly looked at her with her eyes stretched.

"What's wrong?" Tyler asked, suddenly afraid of whatever frightened her friend. "Zoe, speak, you're scaring me. What's wrong?"

"That's him! That's the man who followed me today!"

"Oh my God, Z! He's the Pastor!"

Chapter 3

I Didn't Know It was You!

Zoe pressed her shoulders back against the pew in shock and stared at him with her mouth agape. "Mr. Just a Guy" wasn't just a guy after all. He was the Pastor of the church she had to sing at. She felt butterflies swarm around her stomach. Her mouth went dry and she felt as if she had to make a break for the restroom or she would pee on herself!

"Zoe," Tyler said while jerking Zoe's arm to get her to stand! Zoe slowly looked back at Tyler with her mouth still open. "Come on, he just called us up to sing girl!"

Zoe slowly stood and smoothed her dress in the front and back of her. She was a plus sized woman, but her weight was applied in the right places. She wore that dress like a model! From the looks of the audience when she turned to face them, they confirmed that she did as well.

The sound of Tyler's voice quickly shifted Zoe's mind back to worship. She watched the crowd of people, some with closed eyes, some with lifted hands, and others who just swayed from right to left while they sung. The crowd welcomed them. Just when she thought she could breathe again, "Mr. Just a Guy" came and stood directly in front of her on the front pew. He recognized her and smiled slightly. She smiled nervously, closed her eyes to block him out and kept singing.

Tyler's song was over all too soon. Before she knew it, the musician was playing the introduction to her song. She began to exalt the Lord with her eyes still closed. She began singing. Even with her eyes closed, she could feel his eyes on her. She pressed in the spirit to concentrate on the words of the song to usher the people deeper into worship. She found her place and gave it everything she had. By the time the song was over, sheets were laid over people on the floor. The Pastor was bowed facing the front pew with his back to her. The ushers were fanning people throughout the audience. Tyler had turned her back to the audience and was facing the pulpit in a bent over position. She was so enthralled into worship that her husband was standing over her and trying to wipe her tears.

Zoe was so shocked at the sight before her that it took her even further into worship. This time she sung with her eyes open and praised God for his manifestation in the room. She gave him all of the glory because she was humble enough to know that what took place was all because of him. She was simply his instrument, his spoon that he used to feed the people.

When the song was over, the Pastor was back on his feet facing her. He had a handkerchief in his hand like the one he gave her earlier. He used it to wipe the residue of his tears. Tyler had straightened back up and was facing the audience. She noticed things settling down, so she ended the song and passed the microphone back to the sound guy. He, however, asked her to give that microphone to the Pastor. She reached to pass it to him, and their fingers briefly touched. They made eye contact and she could have sworn she felt a spark. She proceeded to take her seat as he entered the pulpit. He continued to conduct the order of service, but Zoe and Tyler noticed that he couldn't keep his eyes off of her.

Tyler's Pastor finally took the stage and began his sermon. The Pastor, however, kept his eyes on Zoe while uttering an occasional "amen" and "you better preach" to encourage the guest speaker. Zoe did the same, but their eyes continued to lock.

It was so obvious that Tyler elbowed Zoe and mumbled under her breath, "Do you two need to get a room or something?"

Zoe snorted while trying to hold back her laughter. It was the worst thing in the world for Zoe to start laughing in church because she would have a tough time stopping. Zoe gathered herself mentally and focused on her iPad. She then whispered to Tyler to ask the Pastor's name.

"His name is Pastor Thad Wescott," Tyler answered. She looked back up and it was quite obvious that Pastor Wescott was making every effort not to look at Zoe. However, he couldn't help it. Tyler also noticed a woman in her late forties with an all-white, two-piece suit and large hat watching Zoe as well.

She tapped Zoe on her thigh and motioned with her chin in the direction of the woman. Zoe immediately caught her signal and noticed the woman as well. She looked angry and vindictive. She looked like trouble in a church suit. Zoe made a mental note of it and continued to pretend to not notice Pastor Wescott's glances towards her.

The sermon ended, and Tyler's Pastor requested that Tyler and Zoe sing one more song during the altar call. They had to stand within the altar while those requesting prayer stood on the outside of it. This put her in close proximity with Tyler's Pastor and Pastor Wescott. She could smell his cologne from earlier when she passed the microphone to him. This time he intentionally brushed his fingers against hers and looked intently into her eyes while he did it. Zoe stood at 5'4 without heels. With stilettos, she graduated to approximately 5'7. Yet and still, he towered over her with his 6'4 frame. She looked up into his eyes while accepting the microphone with a softly spoken, "thank you."

He nodded and said, "You're welcome."

While this was happening, approximately fifty to sixty people had gathered around the altar. She and Tyler began to harmoniously sing the lyrics to *I Surrender All*.

Zoe was squeezing the microphone so hard her hand hurt. Pastor Wescott stood right behind her. She could feel the warmth of his body heat. She could smell his cologne and he occasionally brushed his arm up against her shoulder while praying for the people. The song seemed to go on forever. She wanted to move. She needed to move. She was too close to him.

Tyler, being as silly as she is, kept making eye contact with Zoe. They spoke without saying a word because they were so in tune with each other. She could tell from Tyler's expression, that she was laughing hysterically on the inside. She, however, fought to compose a straight face. Therefore, she once again closed her eyes so she could focus. When the song was over, she attempted to lay the microphone down on the altar, but it kept rolling. He put his hand on her shoulder to steady himself and reached around her waist to take it from her.

Zoe looked up and behind her to say thank you to him and proceeded to leave the altar. He quickly stepped beside her and took her hand to help her so she wouldn't miss a step and fall.

She took her seat next to Tyler and without moving her lips she said, "Not one word, Tyler. Not one word!" she repeated. Tyler covered her face with the church fan and giggled under her breath.

When the benediction was said, and service was over a caramel colored gentleman, who appeared to be in his twenties, approached Zoe and Tyler. He greeted them both but turned to Zoe.

"Excuse me ma'am," he said, "Pastor Wescott is asking me to escort you to his office. He would like to speak with you."

Zoe's heart dropped and she just knew her legs were shaking. Her already large eyes widened even more, and she looked at Tyler who was snickering like a schoolgirl. Her husband and children had gathered around them in preparation to leave.

Zoe looked back at the young man and gave a brief, "Ok."

She picked up her purse, iPad and car keys while rolling her eyes at Tyler. She waved bye to Tyler's family and proceeded to follow the young man to the Pastor's office. She noticed the woman in all white perched in the corner eyeballing her. When she got up close she smiled and said hello, but the woman rolled her eyes at Zoe. Zoe was taken aback for a moment but quickly got over it.

After taking the stairs to the second floor and making a few turns, they entered the Pastor's office. The scent of his cologne was stationary in the room. She quickly scanned the room. The décor was very masculine and professional. The office furniture was all mahogany wood. The bookshelves were full, and he had a few decorative pieces on the shelves that were eye catching. His desk had a picture of him with two young women. They appeared to be in their early twenties, so she assumed they were his children. He had a bald head and looked way to sexy. She shifted her focus to the plush gray carpet that lined the floor and the two stand up black and gold chairs that sat on the opposite side of his desk.

His chair was very high and had a massager attached to it. She noticed a stainless-steel refrigerator in the corner and a stainless-steel microwave as well. An opened closet held his robes for preaching and a few items of clothing. A door was ajar, and she noticed that it was a bathroom with a shower. The bathroom was black and white to match his office. Her eyes quickly shifted back to the photo of him with the bald head and the shower. "Oh, the things we could do in there while I rub on his…"

Her thoughts were interrupted when she heard the masculine voice say, "You may have a seat here on the couch, ma'am. Pastor Wescott will be with you shortly. Would you like a beverage in the meantime?"

He opened the fridge and she noticed, green tea, water, grape juice, and apple juice. Her throat was feeling dry, but she was so nervous she couldn't bear to even drink anything. Not to mention that he just scared the crap out of her. She quickly shook her head no. The young man nodded towards her respectfully and left the office. As soon as he closed the door, Pastor Wescott entered.

"Good evening young lady." He reached for her hand and she gave it to him. "Small world, huh?"

"Yes, I guess it would be fair to say so."

While still holding her hand and standing over her, he said, "I didn't get to fully introduce myself to you earlier. I wanted the opportunity to do so. I hope that's ok with you."

"Yes of course," she readily said.

"Well then, my name is Thad Wescott and I am the Pastor of this church. May I have the pleasure of knowing your name?"

She was so impressed with his formalities that she stuttered, "Y-yes, my name is Zoe, Zoe Reed."

He unconsciously was rubbing the back of her hand while he held it and she thought she was going to melt!

"Zoe Reed," he repeated, "may I sit next to you?"

"Sure!"

"I must admit, you were on my mind all day after seeing you this morning."

Zoe immediately held her head down a little in embarrassment.

"I promise I'm not usually like that, Pastor Wescott. I was just having a rough day that's all."

He leaned a little closer, "Please, call me Thad."

Zoe nodded in agreement.

"I mean, I've seen people cry before. That's a part of my job as a Pastor, but there was something about you crying that stopped me in my tracks. I prayed for you after meeting you as if I'd known you for years. You mesmerized me, even in your hurt state."

Zoe shifted in her seat. She didn't know what to say. She didn't know if he was flirting with her or extending a helping hand. She decided to just thank him for praying.

"You're welcome. Listen, I really enjoyed your worship! It's been a long time since I've been taken to that place in worship. You can really sing!"

"Thank you," Zoe blushed and said, "to God be the glory."

"That's exactly right. I just have one request from you Zoe and if you say no, I promise I won't be offended."

Zoe sat up a little more in concern. *"What in the world could he want from me,"* she thought?

"I could barely keep my eyes off of you tonight. I know you saw me watching you. I tried not to, but it was simply impossible. You are a very attractive woman Zoe and your anointing only takes it to another level. Would you please do me the honor of accompanying me to dinner?"

Chapter 4

The Age Factor...

If Zoe was one shade lighter than the brown skin she was, she would be as red as an apple. Her almond shaped eyes stretched, and her heart shaped lips smiled nervously. He looked at her like he was about to jump out of his seat with anxiety while waiting for her answer.

"Yes, Pastor Wes...I mean Thad. I'd love to have dinner with you. However, I have one question. How old are you?"

"I'm fifty-one. I'll be fifty-two in December. Is that a problem for you, Zoe? If it is," he took a deep breath and looked at his carpet for a second before lifting his head up to look back at her. "I understand."

"Um, it's not really a problem. I've just never gone a date with someone that much older than me before, let alone a Pastor. This is just different, that's all."

"I understand, Zoe. I know it's impolite to ask a woman's age, but how old are you? I'm thinking you're in your early thirties. Am I right?"

Zoe laughed out loud. "No, I just celebrated my thirty-ninth birthday in June," She glanced at him and noticed that he'd shifted his gaze from her and back to the carpet. "However," she slowly added. "I'm willing to have dinner with you. I mean, although I don't look like I've ever missed a meal, I think I would enjoy your company."

"Zoe, I've always been attracted to women who have a little something extra. From what I can see, your size is perfect. You really are a beautiful woman."

Zoe felt like her face would crack from trying to hide her smile.

He quickly shifted his eyes from the floor back to her and eased back in his seat with his palms on his thigh. "You agreeing to have dinner with me sounds like music to my ears, Zoe. Are you free tomorrow?"

"After I'm done in the salon, I will be. I have a full schedule tomorrow, but I should be able to meet with you by six tomorrow evening."

"Sorry for intruding Pastor," his assistant said as he peeked his head around the door, "but most of the congregation has left and my wife is having a fit because she's pregnant and hungry. May I have one of the ushers wait around for you?"

"No Jamal," Pastor Thad interjected while standing and offering his hand to Zoe so she could stand as well, "go and feed your wife. That's important. We're wrapping up now and we're leaving too."

"Ok Pastor, have a blessed night. Goodnight Sister Zoe," Jamal closed the door as Zoe quickly uttered goodnight to him as well.

"Here's my card once again. May I have the pleasure of obtaining your number as well? Perhaps I can call you to arrange everything."

"Of course!" Zoe reached into her wallet and handed him a card with her information on it, including her picture. He glanced at it and just knew that he would be staring at that photo all night.

"So, you're a preacher?" he asked dumbfounded after reading it on her card.

"Um, yes…Yes I am," she shyly responded.

"Interesting, I'm going to have to talk with you more about that Elder Zoe," he teased.

"Oh Lord, here we go," she said and shook her head at his teasing her. She reached for her purse and he guided her to the door. He turned out the lights and closed his office door behind them. Placing his hand in the middle of her back, Thad led her down the hall and she could've sworn she felt electricity run up her legs from his touch.

Lord please help me cause this man is fine and I already know this is going to be a challenge, she thought to herself. He was talking but she didn't hear a word he'd said. She was so engulfed in his looks, scent, and swag that she just smiled and nodded. They reached the sanctuary, and everyone had left except for maybe five people. An usher, the soundman a few members, and the lady in white.

"Good evening, Pastor Thad. Are you and the visiting Pastor going to waffle house to grab a bite to eat? I'm starving," the lady in all white said with an extremely southern drawl.

Zoe felt Pastor Thad tense up. She glanced up at him as they walked without turning to face her.

His face lost its softness as he replied, "No Sister Yolanda. He's left for the evening and I have other plans."

Sister Yolanda lifted her finger and motioned her mouth to rebut, but he cut her off.

"You get home safe and have a blessed night," He said never looking back at Yolanda as he tightened his grip on Zoe's waist and they continued to walk towards the foyer.

Zoe felt herself giggling like a schoolgirl. She felt like she had won a fight that she didn't willingly invite. Pastor Thad was still quiet as they exited the church.

"Are you ok, Pastor Thad? I'm sorry, I'm just accustomed to referencing titles when at church. My father is a Pastor and I am the same with him. I promise to refer to your first name when we are off the premises."

Zoe seemed to melt his negative energy away. There was something about her that let him know that this would be long term. Their meeting was not by chance. Divine intervention was definitely at play.

"I'm fine, Elder Zoe," he said playfully mocking her by mentioning her title. "Some members just get under my skin and she happens to be one of them. I don't want to end tonight discussing her."

He spotted her car and they continued to walk together.

"So, when will I hear from you regarding our dinner date?" he asked.

"I'll call or text you tomorrow if that's ok," Zoe said as they reached her car and she pressed the unlock button.

Thad opened the door for her and watched as she threw her purse onto the passenger seat then stood before him.

"You don't have to wait until tomorrow. I'd love to talk with you more tonight. If it's ok, can I call you once I get settled in," he asked?

Zoe's smile was bright because she was hoping they could talk more that night as well. "Of course, you can call me tonight. I'll be good in about an hour. It won't take me that long to get home."

"So, if you'll be good in an hour does that mean that your bad right now," he asked and looked at her with a bit of lust in his eyes as he stepped closer?

"Oh my God! Pastor Thad Wescott are you flirting with me?" Zoe was so shocked she didn't know what to say. She just stood there with one hand on her chest and the other on the door of the car.

"I think I am. It's been a while."

Zoe laughed and shook her head in astonishment. "Ok that's it. I'm going home. Call me in an hour, ok?" She eased into the car and put on her seatbelt.

He closed her car door and she put the window down. He reached in and lightly kissed her on the cheek, "Goodnight, Zoe. I'll call you in a few."

Once again, she blushed. "Ok, I look forward to hearing from you."

She started her car and left the church. Once she got out of the parking lot, she was jumping up and down in her seat and screamed with laughter.

"Oh my God, oh my God, oh my God! What just happened? Oh my God!" she kept repeating to herself.

The window was still down, so she leaned back in her seat to enjoy the cool breeze blowing through her curls. She tightened her hand on the steering wheel and stole glances at the sky.

"So, you heard me, huh? Sometimes I don't think you do, but I guess you did this time. Lord, is he the one? This is all so strange. Who would have thought that me crying in the car would get me a date by visiting a church?"

Chapter 5

The Phone Call...

Zoe arrived home within fifteen minutes. She greeted Mr. Hundley then let him out to use the bathroom and stretch his legs a bit. After crating him for the night, she gathered her things and took a quick shower. While showering she pictured his face, smelled his scent, heard his voice and felt his presence. What a powerful presence it was! She quickly shifted her mind because she felt her body responding in a way that it shouldn't.

"Lord," she prayed, "this man is older than me. This is all so new, but if it's you, I'll give it a real chance. Lord, I think this is you though. If it's not, numb my heart. Don't let me feel a thing. I can't handle being hurt again. In Jesus' name I pray, amen. Oh, and Lord, you know my flesh. Please help me not to fall into temptation again. I really want to please you. So, if he is the one, I need to be married asap. In Jesus' name I pray, amen and amen again."

Zoe stepped out of the shower and dried off. She added coconut oil to her hair and body. She then put on an oversized t-shirt and went downstairs. She took her yeti cup from the cabinet and filled it with some lemon flavored alkaline water. She grabbed a banana from the fruit bowl and made her way back upstairs to await Pastor Thad's call. Just as she pulled her peacock designed comforter back, her phone vibrated. It was him! She dug her phone out of her purse and pressed the talk button. She cradled the phone in between her right cheek and shoulder, then climbed into bed.

"Hello Pastor, I mean Thad," she chuckled a little.

"How did you know it was me?"

"Who else would be calling me at this hour?"

"As gorgeous as you are, I'm sure your phone rings all hours of the day and night," he exaggerated.

"Well, first of all, not everyone has the pleasure of having my number and second of all, I don't answer every call!"

"Ok, so I must be special then, huh?"

"Maybe a lil' bit."

They both laughed.

"So, what are you doing? I hope I didn't interrupt you from anything important."

She could hear him shift as if he was getting more comfortable. She was too. She put her charger by the bed just in case her phone threatened to die while she was talking to him.

"No, I actually just got out of the shower and was climbing into bed when you called."

Thad cleared his throat. "Um, Zoe?"

"Yes," she said oblivious to where he was taking the conversation.

"Please don't give me that visual again."

She leaned over in the bed with laughter, "What visual? What are you talking about?" She really felt clueless.

"You mentioned that you just showered and had gotten into bed. If you could only see the picture that flashed in my mind, then you would understand why I just said that."

Zoe burst into laughter. "Thad, you are a mess! I am clothed and in bed. I'm sitting up against my pillow talking to you. I've had a long day so I'm just comfortable sitting in my bedroom."

"Ok, well thank you for clearing that up. I must admit though, I feel like a teenager wanting to ask exactly what you're wearing, but I know that's inappropriate."

She laughed more and said, "Yes, Pastor Thad Wescott, that would be very inappropriate!"

"I know. I'm sorry for bringing it up."

"It's ok."

"So, tell me Zoe, what do you do for fun? Do you have any children? Are you originally from South Carolina?"

"Well, I'm really a simple girl. I love staying at home and watching a good movie. I like walking the beach and sometimes falling asleep on the beach."

"Humph, is that so?"

"Yes."

"The beach is a very exotic place."

"Pastor Wescott," Zoe said in a warning tone while smiling under her breath.

"What? You mentioned sleeping on the beach. A lot can happen on the beach. I'm just saying."

"Ok, Thad, I need you to behave yourself or we're going to have to communicate during the daytime."

"Alright, I'll try."

"So back to what I was saying, I like the park, traveling to various places and I love tasty food. I'm a huge seafood eater! I don't have any children and yes I'm originally from South Carolina."

"Ok, cool. Well, in all seriousness it sounds like we enjoy a lot of the same things. I do have two adult daughters. Ava is twenty-eight and is the CEO of a pharmaceutical company. Autumn is twenty-six and teaches elementary school. They both live in Charlotte."

"Interesting. I hope this doesn't offend you, but do you have any grandchildren? Is there an ex-wife?"

"I'm not offended at all. I don't have any grandchildren yet. Both of my daughters are single, and I am a widower. My wife died in childbirth with Autumn. The doctors never understood how or why she dies. There weren't any complications. Never the less, it's been the girls and I ever since. I've dated a couple of times, but it wasn't serious. My daughters and I are very close, and I guess my focus had always been on them and the church. However, I know that I need to settle down again. Seeing you reminded me of that."

"Is that so?"

"Yes," he smiled into the phone, "does that surprise you?"

"Yeah, it does. You barely know me, yet just the sight of me made you think of settling down?"

"Zoe, I don't think you understand the power that you possess. You are a strikingly beautiful woman. I could see your heart even through your tears. I prayed that you would call me after we met today or that God would allow me to see you again. I gotta tell ya, if you didn't call, I was going to come back to the parking lot of your job to see you!"

"Whatever, no you weren't."

"Yes, I was. I just felt like there was something there. I told you that I prayed for you today. I couldn't shake you from my thoughts. You're something special!"

"Wow! Thank you for praying for me. I was just going through somethings in my mind. I was asking God when things would change for me. Don't get me wrong, I'm doing pretty good for myself but sometimes I want to be held at night. I have a house, I'm a business owner, and I'm educated, but those things can't bring you comfort when you need it."

"Well, Miss Zoe, I'd definitely be willing to hold you but on a serious note," he chuckled. "I understand where you're coming from. Everyone wants to be loved. That's where I am right now in my mind. I'm ready to settle down. I want a wife, someone to travel with, sit next to me in church, and go out to dinner with. I've never been a player. I've always been loyal and that's the kind of person I need. Someone who will be loyal to me too."

"Anyway, Thad," Zoe said as she rolled her eyes at him through the phone. "You're a very attractive guy. I'm sure women flaunt themselves at you every day."

"I won't say every day, but yes, women do approach me. I'm not interested in them though. You, however, caught my eye and my mind! I just knew that there was something to us seeing each other today and again tonight! Things like that just don't happen."

"Perhaps you're right. Oh, and don't think I forgot about that sly remark regarding you holding me. You're a fresh Pastor!" Zoe buckled over onto the other side of the bed in laughter.

Thad covered his mouth with his hand so she wouldn't hear him laughing.

"I mean," Thad thought for a moment. "I am who I am Zoe. I am a Pastor, but I am very human! I'm also very honest. This is another reason why I'm asking the Lord to send me a wife. I haven't been perfect, but it is my goal to abstain from sex until marriage. That doesn't mean that I won't flirt with you. It also doesn't mean that I won't be tempted. However, I'm putting my best foot forward to hold on until my wedding night. With you being a preacher, I'm sure you're ok with that, right?"

"Of course, I'm ok with that. I have rough moments too but I'm not trying to be on the altar for fornicating. It's not always easy, however, I do believe it will be worth it."

"If you marry me, it will! I can guarantee you that!"

"Is that so?" Zoe asked.

"That's definitely so!"

Zoe continued laughing and they talked until Zoe noticed the time.

"Oh my God, Thad it's two in the morning! I can't believe we've been on the phone this long."

He made her laugh until her stomach hurt. She loved a man with a good sense of humor and he loved a woman who could laugh at his jokes.

"No way it's that late…or should I say early. I'm going to let you go. Do you work tomorrow?"

"Yes, my first client won't arrive until ten o' clock, so I'll be ok. I do need to get some sleep though. Today was exhausting."

"Ok, well I'd love to see you again. Will you be free tomorrow evening?"

"Um, yes, I'll be free around six tomorrow."

"Ok, maybe I can take you to dinner? You did promise me a date."

"Yes, I know, and I do keep my promises, Pastor Wescott."

"Girl don't be saying my name all sexy like that at this hour. You're about to awaken a beast!"

"You are crazy," she bellowed in laughter. "That's it, I'm getting off this phone with you right now. You are too much!"

He laughed a little as well, "So where will we meet at or are you ok with me picking you up?"

"I'm ok with you picking up. I normally would meet a person somewhere, but I trust you. I'll text you my address. What type of restaurant will we be going to? I don't want to overdress."

"Is seafood ok with you?"

"Yes! I love seafood!"

"Ok, great. It will be somewhere downtown and maybe we can get some gelato afterwards."

"Alright, that sounds wonderful."

"So, six tomorrow it is. I'm gonna let you go for real this time. Have a good night, ok?"

"You too, Thad. Goodnight."

Zoe just knew that someone was playing a cruel joke on her. There was no way this was happening. Today would be marked in history as the most emotionally unstable, yet great day, she's had in a long time. She turned out the light on her nightstand and slid under the covers. She caught herself smiling. She glanced over at the vacant pillow alongside of her and sighed.

"God, is this really happening? I feel like a teenager. It's been years since I've been able to just talk with a man over the telephone. Lord, you know my flesh though. I'm going to need your help. I don't need to hide anything from you because you already know my thoughts. Lord, Thad is fine! Help me not to fornicate please. If he's the one Lord, we have to get married soon. Help me to guard my heart in the meantime though."

She dozed off to sleep.

***

8AM came all too soon for Zoe. She got out of bed, prayed and went through her usual routine. She grabbed her phone and went downstairs to make a cup of coffee and greet Hundley too. He was happy to see her as usual. While her coffee brewed, she checked her phone. The first text message of the day was her client confirming her appointment. She replied back. The second text message was from Thad.

Thad: Good morning, beautiful. I slept better last night than I have in years. I really enjoyed talking to you. I hope you have a wonderful day. See you soon and please remember to text me your address.

Zoe smiled as she read it but panicked in her mind because she forgot to text him her address. She texted him back immediately.

Zoe: Good morning Thad. I enjoyed talking with you as well. See you soon and have a great day.

She included her address in the text and hit the send button. Zoe leaned on the counter with the phone pressed against her chest and smiled as she stared up at the ceiling. The beeping of the coffee pot startled her, and she turned to pour herself a cup. She let Hundley out of his crate and of course he was happy to be able to jump all over her. She just smiled, took her cup of coffee upstairs and pulled out something simple for work. As she was walking upstairs to her bedroom, her phone beeped. It was Thad texting her. She stopped on the stairs to read his text. She was smiling before she even knew what it said. It had been a while since she'd received this much attention.

Thad: For a moment, I thought you'd changed your mind when I didn't get your text about the address last night. Thanks for responding to me this morning. I'm grinning from ear to ear. Talk with you later.

Zoe: Sir, I'm just as excited as you are. I apologize for not texting right away. I forgot just that quick and then I fell asleep. Please forgive me.

Thad: No apologies necessary, dear. See you soon ok.

Zoe: Ok.

Zoe proceeded upstairs and prepared for her day. She decided to wear a pair of blue jeans with a black V-neck t-shirt that read, *Hair Stylists Rock*. She put on champagne colored lipstick and large gold hoop earrings. It was the perfect color for her hazelnut complexion. She fluffed her natural curls and added a part in the middle of her head. She slid on her Nike flip flops and headed out to work. Zoe drove to work in confidence that day. She was smiling with excitement, and for once in a long time — she felt good about herself. She bopped her head to the music playing on the radio and tapped her fingers on the steering wheel. There was hardly any traffic on the road due to it being Saturday. She arrived to work within less than fifteen minutes.

Chapter 6

Who Sent those...

As soon as Zoe got into the salon, she turned on some contemporary gospel music and danced a little as she prepared her station. Tyler came in shortly after she did and was giggling as she entered the salon.

"You're feeling good today I see. Girl, Pastor Wescott couldn't keep his eyes off of you last night! How did things go after we left?"

"Whatever, Tyler. It was not that serious!" Zoe put on her smock and sat in her styling chair and waited for her first client to arrive.

"I don't know who you think you're fooling. That man looked like he wanted to end service and take you in the back for a little personal prayer-time and laying on of the hands." Tyler winked at Zoe as she unpacked her bag and prepared her station.

Zoe played with her curls by twisting them around her finger and swinging her chair in a half circle. "Okay, okay. He was watching me, and I must admit, it was flattering. He had me come to his office and he basically told me that he's attracted to me."

Tyler flopped into her chair and giggled like a thirteen-year-old girl. "He did not!"

"Yeah, he did Ty. I was in shock because out of all the years that I've been in church, I've never experienced anything like this before! He's a bit older than me though."

"Zoe, but he's so fine! Forget his age, I could so see you two together. Shucks, I could feel the chemistry between you two while we were doing praise and worship. I was like, 'let me get out of these people's way'."

Zoe laughed. "Ty, I thought I was going to pass out when he stood next to me. He smelled so good and his presence is just overwhelming. It's like he commands your attention just by being near you."

Just then, the door to the salon opened. Zoe didn't see a face, but she saw this huge bouquet of orange and white lilies.

The person holding the flowers said, "Good morning, I'm looking for Zoe." The delivery guy's eyes wandered between Tyler and Zoe.

A few of the other stylists entered the salon at the same time. The bouquet was so big he struggled holding it. They stopped and stared at the bouquet with smiles on their faces and wonder as well. They wanted to know who the flowers were for and who sent them. They had clients on the way, so they proceeded to their stations to prepare but still watched to see who the delivery guy was there for.

"I—I'm Zoe," she stuttered and raised her hand to get his attention. "You can set them here," she said as she pointed to the empty spot on her station. He walked over to her and sat the flowers down.

"Have a good day ma'am and enjoy your flowers."

"Wait, let me give you a tip," she said and reached for her purse.

"That's not necessary ma'am, the sender has already taken care of that," he smiled and left the salon.

Tyler and Zoe's clients must've ridden in together, because they walked into the salon right behind each other. Zoe put her purse away and asked her client to have a seat at her station. Tyler told her client the same thing and rushed over to Zoe.

"Hurry up and read the card girl! I'm about to pass out from excitement," Tyler rushed Zoe.

"Okay! Okay!" She reached between the orange and white lilies and opened the cream-colored envelope. The card was orange with gold glitter on it. It had an orange lily on the top left corner. Zoe smiled at the theme of it all then she read the card loud enough for only Tyler to hear. "I can't wait to see that beautiful smile of yours tonight. I pray that your day is tremendously blessed. Sincerely, Thad."

Zoe pressed the card to her chest and looked at Tyler. Tyler's mouth was opened in a state of shock.

"Zee, he's something serious, honey!"

"I know! I don't even know what to say. This is all surreal to me."

"Um, Ms. Zoe, come on and spill the tea! Who's giving you flowers ma'am," one of the stylists asked while the others, who came in while she read the card, chimed in as well?

"Just some guy that I met yesterday. It's nothing serious y'all."

"Nothing serious?" Another stylist quizzed with her hand on her hip and a comb in the other as she waved in the air.

"No, we just met yesterday, and we have a date today. I guess he's just generous," Zoe said and shrugged her shoulders and placed the card in her purse.

"Well, it sounds like this dude is ready for something serious. Men don't go around sending flowers before the date! Heck they barely send them afterwards from my experience," Tyler's client blurted out and rolled her eyes while she said it.

"Chile please, spreading your legs in the back of a run-down Neo Sport doesn't classify as a date. That's why you don't get any flowers," Zoe's client said teasingly.

Tyler's client sucked her teeth and flipped through a nearby magazine without a response.

"Alright y'all, that's enough. Let's get some coconut oil on these strands and some curl patterns popping on these heads," Zoe jumped in before the conversation got too serious. She didn't tolerate gossip or derogatory jokes in her salon.

All the stylists went to work but everyone kept eyeing Zoe and her flowers, including Tyler. Zoe and Tyler shampooed and conditioned their clients, then put them under the dryers at the same time.

"Zoe, come with me," Tyler said and grabbed Zoe's hand to take her into the laundry room.

"Zee, he is really feeling you! How do you feel? Are you excited?"

"Yeah, she slowly let out. I'm excited, nervous, scared and that's just a few of the emotions that I'm feeling right now. We really hit it off over the phone, Tyler. We didn't hang up until after two this morning. I didn't want to end the call. I haven't felt this way in a long time. I don't want to say he's the one though because it's too soon. I'm just going to take it slow, but girl, my flesh is weak. I was doing good until I met him and now sex is all I'm thinking about. I mean, he's intriguing but he's sexy too!"

"Ok Zee, I think we're gonna have to fast and pray. Do we need to use some spiritual gorilla glue to keep those panties up?" Tyler joked.

"Yeah, I just might need that, Ty!"

They both laughed and went back to the salon to check on their clients. The day went by fast for everyone except Zoe. She couldn't wait to see Thad. She kept thinking about their talk, how he smelled, the sound of his voice, and the way her body felt electrified when he touched her back. She found herself in a daze. Slowly but surely, her day came to an end and she was back at home. She didn't dare leave her flowers either. She brought them home with her and sat them on her dining room table. Zoe stood in her closet and was at a loss as she pondered what to wear. Although she was a preacher, she couldn't figure out how to dress to go on a date with one!

She called Tyler to get advice. Tyler reminded her that Pastor Wescott is still a man and she's still a woman, although they are both preachers. She told her to dress like she would for any other date. Zoe showered off her workday and settled on some blue denims that were quite fitted and a royal blue wrap blouse. The knot of the blouse tied in the middle and the end of the blouse had a slight hint of a ruffle. It had a quarter length sleeve and showed enough cleavage to flirt, but not to come off like a harlot. She put on some denim and beige strapped wedges, gold earrings, bracelets and reapplied her champagne lipstick.

Just as she spritzed on her perfume, Mr. Hundley started barking to alert her of someone's presence at the door. Soon after he barked, the doorbell rang. She waived her wrists so her perfume would dry quickly and ran downstairs to the door. She looked through the peephole and verified that it was him. When she opened the door, you could feel the electricity between the two of them. She took his breath away and she felt as if she immediately needed something cold to drink. She would have to fast and pray right away if she was going to remain celibate!

Chapter 7

The Date...

"You look amazing, Zoe!" Thad smiled. He had another set of white lilies in his hand and presented them to her. He hugged her briefly and took a step back.

"Thank you, Thad! You look great yourself. Thad wore light blue jeans with a long sleeved white shirt and some brown slip on shoes.

Thank you so much for the flowers from earlier and now," she reached for them and stepped aside for him to come in. "If you don't mind, I'd like to put these in some water before we leave. You can have a seat if you'd like.

"Ok, that's cool," he said as he walked toward the sofa while keeping his eyes on her. She walked like a lioness. Every curve caught his attention. She was plus sized, and he desired nothing less.

Zoe turned around and looked at him while watering the flowers. "Thad!"

"Huh?" he snapped out of his zone when she said his name with urgency.

"Did you hear me?"

"No. Uh, I'm sorry. What did you say?"

Zoe dried her hands with a paper towel, threw it in the garbage can and sashayed her way back over to him. Hand on her hip, she said, "I was asking if you've been to this restaurant before." she giggled nervously because the look in his eyes told her that he would have preferred not to leave the house.

"Yeah, I've been there once or twice before."

"Were you there on a date?"

"No ma'am, absolutely not," he said while shaking his head from side to side like a nine-year old boy. "I was there on business."

"Ok. I gotcha. Let me grab my purse from upstairs and we can go," Zoe hurried upstairs.

As she went, so did his eyes and his mind. He wished he could go upstairs too.

"Dude, snap out of it! You've held on this long. Don't mess up now," he said to himself. "Lord, I'm really liking Zoe. Please tell me if she's my wife. I can't waste my time or hers. I feel like she's mine, but I need to hear it from you. Lord, if I can't hear you because of my own ideas then please send a prophet. I just need to know."

At this point, he was unconsciously pacing the floor of her living room and rubbing his hands together as he mumbled this prayer to the Lord. Zoe startled him when she appeared again in bubbly formation.

She grabbed her keys from the key rack, "Are you ready?"

"Sure, or we could hang out here if you'd like." he said with a sly grin.

"Uh-uh, no sir, let's go!"

They both laughed a little as they walked towards the door. Zoe set the alarm and they proceeded outside to his Maybach. He opened her door and she sat in the seat. He instinctively leaned in and reached over her to put on her seatbelt.

Zoe yelped. "Thad, what in heaven's name are you doing?" She thought she was going to die right there. He was too close to her. His cologne sat in her nostrils.

"What?" he asked innocently.

"What are you doing?" she proceeded to lean further back in the seat and put her hands up in the front of her breasts.

"I was trying to put on your seatbelt," he said as he backed away and looked at her. This is right after she heard the seatbelt click and realized he was telling the truth.

Zoe shook her head in embarrassment and rolled her eyes. "Sorry, Thad. You just freaked me out for a second. I didn't know what was happening."

He reached in again and kissed her cheek. "It's ok."

He then walked around to the driver's side. He laughed a little to himself while stealing glances of her.

"You wanna tell me what's so funny, Pastor Wescott?"

He straightened his face right away and said, "There you go with that Pastor stuff and sure, I'll tell you. I was laughing because you talked all that trash on the phone, but when I reached in to buckle your seatbelt, you almost had a stroke!"

"Don't flatter yourself! I just didn't know what you were doing," she said matter-of-factly. "I've been putting on my own seatbelt for the past thirty-nine years so that was just different for me."

"Yeah, I hear ya."

She popped his arm and they both relaxed as they enjoyed the scenery while listening to the soft sound of jazz playing in the background. They made light conversations on the way to the restaurant. They both were more nervous and excited than they revealed.

When they arrived at the restaurant, the valet opened Thad's door and took his keys. Thad rushed to Zoe's door and opened it for her. She unbuckled her seatbelt before he reached in again and caused her to feel her heart leap out of her chest. He reached for her hand to help her out of the car.

"Man do you smell good!" He said it before he thought about it what he was saying. Never the less, he wasn't taking it back. "You smell edible," he whispered into her ear then gave the hostess his name. They followed the hostess to a corner table with a clear view of King Street. Thad's hand was on the small of her back the entire time. Zoe had to inwardly pray for strength and so did Thad!

Once the hostess left, the server appeared.

"Good evening, Mr. Wescott and Ms. Reed. What will you be having to drink this evening?"

Zoe ordered a strawberry lemonade and Thad ordered an Arnold Palmer. As soon as the server walked away, Zoe asked about the Arnold Palmer.

"What's an Arnold Palmer, Thad? Is it alcoholic?"

"No, of course not. It's sweet tea and lemonade mixed together."

"Oh, ok. It seems like I've heard it called something similar to that but now that I think about it, it was just mispronounced. Oh, and Sir, did you really say that I smelled edible?" Zoe looked astonished that those words actually left his lips.

"Yes, I did. Did I offend you?" He looked up from the menu to look into her eyes.

"No, not at all. I was just taken aback that you said it, that's all."

"I was only being honest. You smell like coconut, vanilla, and something else that I can't quite place, but it all smells edible none the less."

Zoe had no response. She just shook her head and tried to read the menu.

"What? You have nothing to say, Elder Reed?"

Zoe kept looking at the menu but laughed while pretending to ignore him.

"So, you're going to ignore me?"

Zoe continued ignoring him. He yanked the menu from the table, and she laughed even harder.

"What, Thad?"

"You need to get your mind out of the gutter, that's what! I was just saying that you smell like fruity items."

Zoe didn't say anything. She just looked at him and smirked.

"Okay, I guess it came out wrong, but I really wasn't trying to be fresh."

Zoe still didn't say anything.

"Shucks, here's your menu back. You've got jokes tonight."

Zoe graciously looked at the menu again and they both laughed while contemplating what they would eat. The server came back with their drinks and they ordered their food. They both ordered a broiled seafood platter which consisted of shrimp, flounder, scallops and oysters. They both had red rice and steamed vegetables as their side items. Thad held her hand as he said grace and they ate. They made small talk throughout the meal. However, Thad couldn't stop noticing how beautiful she really was. He noticed the curl pattern of her hair, the twinkle in her eyes when she laughed, and the slight dimple in her right cheek. He surely noticed how she slightly teased him with her neckline as well. He'd give anything to be the blouse she was wearing right now. He noticed everything about her and on her. He loved all of it. Dinner ended, and the valet was back with Thad's vehicle.

"Would you like to walk the park and hang out by the water? It's a full moon, so I'm sure it's gorgeous tonight."

"I'd love that!" Zoe agreed.

He opened the door and let her in. She sat back and waited for him to come in and buckle her seatbelt. He noticed her position and leaned in to secure her. He moved slowly but on purpose. He knew that his presence was enticing to her. He was reveling in her being uncomfortable and knowing that she wanted him, just as much as he wanted her. When he backed away, he stopped for a moment and looked her square in the eyes. He didn't say a word or make a move. He saw her hold her breathe. However, he was calm. His movements were timed and intentional. He then lifted one eyebrow, smiled lightly, licked his lips, and backed out of the vehicle. When he closed the door, Zoe let out her breathe and placed her palm on her chest. He, on the other hand was chuckling to himself as he walked to the driver side of the car.

He got in and said, "May I hold your hand?"

She gave him her left hand and he drove away from the restaurant heading for the park. Every now and then, he stroked the back of her hand with his thumb. Zoe leaned her head against the headrest and enjoyed the view of the lights on King street, as well as the privilege of his touch. She admired the height of the buildings, the variation of colors, the recent renovations, and the stories some of the older buildings told with its aged look. She suddenly appreciated this moment more than ever. She was with a man that she really liked, and the feeling was mutual. Sex wasn't in the midst of it. It may have been on their minds, but not in their sin bucket.

"Someone's in deep thought," he said and jolted Zoe from her tranquil place.

"I'm just enjoying the moment."

He gave her a kind glance and parked the vehicle near the sidewalk. The tide was so high that they could see the water from where they sat. He reached for her hand again and cracked the windows.

"Would you like to walk? You look pretty relaxed right now and I don't want to disturb that."

"We can walk if you'd like to. I'm ok either way."

"Are you always so easy going, Zoe?"

She pondered his question for a moment and then responded with a sharp. "Nope!"

They both laughed at her honesty.

"I'm just kidding. For the most part, I'd have to say yes. I'm pretty easy going. I don't require a lot. Simple things make me happy," she said as she tilted her head and body to the side to get a better view of his face.

"That's good to know because I like doing big things for the people I care about. God has blessed me in so many ways that I just can't afford to be selfish. I believe in giving back."

"Give me an example."

"Well, like the flowers that I sent to your job. I knew you weren't expecting them, so I figured I'd send the biggest bouquet available. You probably thought that because I sent those that I wouldn't bring anything tonight when I picked you up, so I brought them. I just like putting a smile on your face."

"Why? You just met me."

"I don't know why. It's been a long time since I've felt anything this severe for a woman since my wife passed away. I'm just really drawn to you. I probably shouldn't be telling you this, but you could probably ask me for anything, and I'd give it to you within reason. It feels like I've known you for years. Like, there's a connection between us that's crazy. It's really strong," he took her hand into his and kissed it lightly.

Zoe felt her body shudder.

"Does that scare you, Zoe?"

She cleared her throat and noticeably shifted in her seat. "Um, no, it doesn't scare me per se. It makes me a little nervous, but it doesn't scare me."

"Why does it make you nervous?"

"I guess because you're right. The chemistry between us is something serious! I've had men who liked and loved me, but, I'm not interested in a boyfriend. I want to be married. My prayer is that, whomever I spend time with, for the Lord to reveal quickly if they are to be my husband or not."

He rubbed his thumb over her hand again and her body tingled even more. She lightly bit her bottom lip and closed her eyes. She opened them quickly when she realized that she was telling on herself.

He was looking her directly in the face and she looked away. She tried to ease her hand from his grip, but he only tightened it.

"Thad!"

"Zoe!"

She laughed and tried to pull her hand away again, but he wouldn't let her.

"May I have my hand back please?"

"No," he proceeded to kiss her hand again.

She breathed deeply because of the excitement he was causing. She snatched her hand away and reached for the door handle. The door was locked.

"Thad, unlock the door. Please."

"Why?"

He reached for her hand again, but she tucked it under her thigh.

"Do you really think that I'm afraid to pull your hand from under there?"

"Unlock the door, Thad!" Zoe was laughing so of course he didn't take her serious at all.

"Are you ready to walk?

"We don't have to walk but I need to get some air."

"Ok," he lowered the window further. "Is that enough air for you."

Zoe popped him on the arm. "Thad stop playing. Can we exit the car, please?"

Thad answered by putting the windows up and unlocking the doors. He got out of the vehicle and came around to open her door. Just as he neared her side, she was half of the way out of the car. He blocked her in between the door of the car and her seat. They stood face to face.

"Why are you opening your own door?"

"I didn't think it was a problem."

"If I'm going to be your man," he said and stepped closer to her, placing his hands on her waist. "You're going to have to let me be the man!"

Zoe was pretty sure she stopped breathing and was standing at the pearly gates. She didn't say anything. She couldn't move. She didn't know what to say or what to do. This man was older, and he had a swag about himself that demanded her to oblige. His height and size seemed to suffocate her. Any other time, she'd have something sarcastic to say but she couldn't think of anything at this moment.

He lifted her chin with his finger. "Do you hear me, Elder Zoe Reed?"

"Yes, Pastor Thad Wescott, I hear you."

"I'm going to change your name ma'am," he backed away and gave her room to move.

She sighed with relief that he moved out of her personal space.

"Is that so?"

"It sure is," he took her hand again, but he leaned on the car once he closed the door. She stood in the front of him and challenged him with her eyes.

"It certainly is. I don't plan on being single much longer. Heck, I can't be single much longer while around you!"

"What's that supposed to mean?"

"It means that if I'm going to stay saved, I need to be married, so I'm not on the altar as a fornicator."

Zoe backed away and laughed. "I understand, Thad. I'm not trying to fornicate either. God has kept me for a while now. I want to continue to be kept but you Sir, have to behave yourself."

"Me?"

"Yes, you."

"Do you really find me attractive, Zoe? I know I'm older than you and we're both praying for the same things, which is a spouse. However, I really need to know what you think of me." he reached for her hand again.

She looked away at the sidewalk. Strangers walked by holding hands and whispering to each other. She looked further down the sidewalk and noticed couples leaning on the rails giving brief kisses. She also noticed couples on the benches of the park who were cuddling and felt her heart become heavy but happy at the same time. Thad noticed the look on her face. He also saw what she saw. He wanted what she wanted but he had to know if she wanted it with him. He felt like he knew it, yet he needed her to say it.

"Ma'am, are you going to answer me?"

"Yes." She swung her free hand behind her back and twisted her body from side to side. She looked like a little girl while doing it.

"Yes, you're going to answer me or yes you're attracted me?" he licked his bottom lip and Zoe thought her knees would buckle beneath her.

She blinked hard and said, "Yes, Thad. I do find you attractive. Very attractive I should say." she suddenly felt bold and stepped closer to him.

It was his turn to hold his breathe and feel as if the ground was about to give out. Women came on to him all the time, but none who really piqued his interest. She rubbed his hand the way he rubbed hers and looked into his eyes as well.

"I thought you were attractive when we met. I just didn't think you'd be into me because of my voluptuousness." This time, she licked her lips.

Thad's heart raced inside of his chest. This woman was fine, sexy, smart, saved, had her own things and she was winning him over by the second. He stood up from the car and that made him closer to her. She didn't step back either. She met him where he stood. His reaction, however, was unexpected.

He let her hand go and this time, instead of touching her waist, he wrapped his arms around her waist. "Ms. Reed, I've told you before and I'll say it as many times as you need to hear it. I love your size. I love your curves." His hands lingered on her lower back but slightly on her butt. "I love all of what I see. I don't want you to lose a pound. I think you're very attractive, every inch of you."

At that moment she felt every inch of him too! He leaned in closer and his nose touched hers. She licked her lip again and the light bulb clicked on in his head. He jerked his hand away and stepped back. He adjusted his shirt over his pants and put his hands in his pockets to fill his pants out more.

"With that being said, maybe we should call it a night. What I'm feeling right now could get the both of us in trouble with God."

He didn't wait for her to respond. Instead, he stepped aside and opened the door for her to get into the car. Zoe got in and sat straight up with a ere of confidence. She was going to enjoy this man!

Thad, once again, reached in and locked her seatbelt. She didn't flinch. She showed no signs of nervousness. She looked in his face as if she was daring him to make a move. He laughed and rubbed his chin while backing out of the car.

"This woman is going to be something else. I already see it," he mumbled to himself.

She reached over and opened his door for him. He'd never had a woman to do such a simple gesture for him. He entered the vehicle and thanked her. She responded by reaching for his hand. Once he started the vehicle and pulled from the parking spot, he gave her his hand and they both sat silently, just enjoying the ride.

"I feel like some ice cream. Would you like some ice cream, Zoe?"

"Sure, but only if you let me treat you this time."

"Ok. I can get with that."

They went to a gelato and ice cream shop in the market. She got gelato and after he got a sample, he decided on gelato too. They walked the market and ate their gelato at the same time, admiring the African American markers of history on the brick walls. They discussed slavery and where America stands today regarding racism. They enjoyed the live music being played on the streets and the view of baskets being weaved as the patrons made their purchases. Soon, the gelato was gone, and their hands were locked in once again. They walked and talked as if they'd been together for years. It certainly felt like it. It felt as if they were made for each other. They both knew that God was amidst them. They were just going to have to fight to keep it holy.

Zoe felt at peace as he drove her home. She really didn't want the night to end but they both had church the next day. They arrived at her home and he quickly walked to her side of the car to open her door. She stepped out and they were quiet as she went to open her garage door. Mr. Hundley could be heard from the outside with his barking.

She unlocked the door to her home and turned to face him. "It's been a great evening," she yelled over Mr. Hundley. Thad started to respond when she interrupted him. "Would you mind coming in so I can quiet him down?

"Sure, no problem," he stepped into the laundry room of her home and into the kitchen behind her. He turned and hit the alarm on his car as she pressed the button to close her garage door.

She let Mr. Hundley out after making sure Thad was ok with dogs. He ran to him and Thad gave him his hand to smell. Mr. Hundley barked a few more times and then went back to his doggy bed. Finally, he was quiet.

"Why didn't he bark like that when I came in the first time?"

"He barked to let me know you were outside, but he was also in the middle of a nap, so he quieted down right after you came inside. Once he knows that I'm ok, he normally stops. Do you have any pets?"

"No, not anymore. I had an American bulldog once, but my daughter took him with her to Charlotte. I got so busy with the church that I didn't have time for him, so I gave him to her to care for. He's about fifteen years old now in dog years."

"Oh, cool."

"Well, Zoe, I really enjoyed myself tonight," he stepped closer to where she stood near the refrigerator.

"I did too."

"Do you think we could do this again soon?"

"Yes, just say when."

"We only have one church service tomorrow and I'm not preaching in the morning. We have a guest speaker coming in. We normally get out of church around 1pm. Would you like to have lunch or dinner?"

"That's fine. We can do either. Our services begin at eight, so I'm free after that."

"Really? Well, how would you feel about coming to my church at eleven to do a praise and worship for me? My praise team would be glad for the break and my congregation really enjoyed you. I saw a few of the live videos on Facebook."

"Ok, I think I could do that. I normally get approval from my Pastor first but being that I was just there on Friday, I'm sure he'll be ok with it."

"Alright, well, I'll let you go. I'll see you tomorrow."

"Ok."

He stepped closer and kissed her partly on her cheek and her ear. He heard her moan and slowly backed away. He held his lips there for a moment as he took in her sent one last time for the night.

"Good night, Ms. Reed."

"Good night, Mr. Wescott."

She opened the laundry door and the garage door. She stood and watched him back out of her driveway before she closed the garage door. She stepped back into the house, kicked off her heals and did a quick dance as if she had drums and a keyboard backing her up. She glanced at the clock and noticed that it was 10pm. She ran to the phone to text Tyler.

Zoe: Hey girlie, the date was off the chain. He asked me to do P & W tomorrow at 11 and we will go out after that. I can't wait to tell you all of the details. Ttyl Gn.

She didn't care about errors. Tyler knew exactly what she was saying. Before she could head upstairs, her phone beeped alerting her of a text message.

Thad: I miss you already. How could this be when we've just met? See you tomorrow. Sweet dreams beautiful.

Her phone beeped again. This time it was Tyler.

Tyler: Hey girl! OMG. I can't wait to hear about this! I know you were cute! Call me tomorrow after your first service.

She texted Tyler back first but waited a few minutes to text Thad. Her mother always taught her not to come off to available.

Zoe to Tyler: lol and ok.

Zoe to Thad: the feeling is definitely mutual. See you tomorrow and sweet dreams to you as well.

Chapter 8

The Prophecy...

She clutched the phone to her chest and skipped upstairs like a little girl. She ran and fell onto her bed. She just stared at the ceiling as if she could see through it, pass the clouds and into the heavens.

She prayed. "God, what are you up to? Are your hands really in this? Is this really you working for me? God I can't handle another counterfeit. This seems real to me. Lord, I really need confirmation that this is you and not my flesh wanting what it wants."

She sat up in the bed and let her feet dangle from the end of the it. She felt tears swelling in her eyes.

"Lord, I've messed up so many times before. I've fornicated knowing that it was wrong. I know that my actions don't always show it, but Lord I really do love you. I just want to make the right moves. I can't go back to standing at the altar because I've messed up the night before. Lord, I've been embarrassed so many times in the past because I brought someone to church with me, and later, it didn't work. I don't want to go through that again."

She wiped a tear that spilled from her eye and ran down her cheek.

"Church people can be so judgmental and with me being the Pastor's daughter, I don't want to bring a reproach upon my parents or my church. Lord, I know I keep repeating myself but please Jesus, if he's not the one, please bring this to a swift end. I only want who and what you want me to have. Speak Lord. I need to hear from you."

She got up and prepared for a shower to ease her mind. As the water from the shower flowed, so did her tears. She needed an answer from the Lord. She wanted to be married but she just met him. How long would they even court? There was no way she could be around this man for two to three years and not have sex. They would have to have chaperoned dates or something.

"Lord, my life is in your hands. Help me to rest in you, Father. Help my unbelief," she whispered to the Lord as she dried off. Zoe put on her pajamas and turned on the television until she drifted off to sleep.

***

At six a.m., her alarm was chiming in her ear. Zoe got up and prepared for church. She would be attending hers and Thad's church. She decided on a red asymmetrical top that flowed to her ankles in the back but stopped at her waist in the front. She added a black pencil skirt to go with it, a pair of black sheer stockings and her black stilettos. She added a simple silver necklace, bracelet, earrings and her watch as accessories. She didn't forget to grab a lap scarf to cover her legs. It was black with a hint of sparkle in the lace trimming. She decided to let her natural curls hang out today. Smoothing her edges, she spritzed her hair with a little water, leave in conditioner and coconut oil. Her level 4c coiled hair was on point. She didn't have to do much with it but if she chose to, then she had the versatility to do so.

She sprayed on her perfume, grabbed her bible, an extra pair of flats and headed downstairs. She took care of Mr. Hundley, grabbed a protein drink and by 7:30am, she was headed to her church. As usual, when she arrived, she was on duty. Her parents depended on her a lot. Therefore, she tried her best to always be in place naturally and spiritually. She didn't always succeed but she did make the attempt. She, of course led praise and worship and the power of the Lord moved through the audience to the point that her Pastor could barely preach. Never the less, he got through it. The makeup that she had applied before she left this morning was gone! She was thankful that she traveled with her make up bag.

Church was jumping by the time her Pastor finished preaching. The altar was packed with unbelievers, those who just needed a touch from the Lord, and the Sunday altar repeater (those who come to the altar every Sunday but go right back to the same thing on Monday). Her Pastor laid his hands on the people and his wife followed suit. People were laid out on the floors, dancing in the isles, and Kleenex was everywhere. It was just something to behold. Her Pastor startled her when he called her name in the microphone.

"Elder Zoe, come here daughter."

She went up and stood before her Pastor.

"The Lord told me to tell you — man this is hard for me as your Father — but the Lord told me to tell you that you are getting married soon. He said he hasn't forgotten about you. He said the person you've been praying about is the one. He said trust him and he'll get you through the process."

Zoe started to dance but just as she did, he tapped her on her shoulder.

"That's not all, Elder. The Lord said that your marriage is going to take place soon. You will not be single much longer!"

Zoe, the Pastor, and his wife along with most of the congregation broke out into a dance. Her brother deserted the keyboard and came to dance with her. She cried and danced and danced and cried. God sent the word that she needed to hear. She felt like she could fly. God had heard her cry and her prayer. He is doing just what he said he would do. By the time she left church it was 10:45am. She touched up her makeup when she got in the car and proceeded to Thad's church.

"Lord, you actually came through. You spoke to me prophetically about what I just prayed about. Thank you, Lord. I love you, Father."

Before she knew it, she was turning into the parking lot of Pastor Thad's church. The parking lot attendant must've been looking out for her car because he had her park right next to Pastor Thad's car. He opened her door for her and assisted her with exiting the vehicle.

"God bless you, Elder Reed. I'm Elder Rollins. Pastor Thad asked me to escort you to the prayer room and then we'll go into the sanctuary."

"Ok, great."

They entered the building and went into the prayer room. There was Pastor Thad, who immediately rushed over to greet her with a friendly hug.

He leaned in and whispered in her ear, "You look gorgeous! Let me introduce you to our ministerial staff."

He took pride in introducing her to the other Elders, Prophets, Evangelists and the praise team of his congregation.

"Ladies and gentlemen, this is Elder Zoe Reed. She'll be doing praise and worship for us today.

"Oh my God, Elder Reed, we really enjoyed you on Friday night! The oil on your life is real honey," one of the leaders chimed in!

"Thank you," Zoe said as she muffled a laugh. "To God be the glory!"

A few amens came from around the room and a few others chimed in as well regarding her praise and worship from Friday night.

"Well, let's pray," said Pastor Thad.

They all formed one big circle and held hands. Pastor Thad led the prayer and Zoe had to open her eyes to look at him. He prayed so hard it felt like they had just had another church service!

This man is anointed! Lord, you're giving him to me? Zoe asked the Lord rhetorically.

When the prayer was over, hallelujahs and amens filled the room. They left the prayer room and headed to the sanctuary together. Zoe followed with Pastor Thad in tow.

"Would you like to sit in the pulpit with me, Zoe?" Thad asked while adjusting his jacket as they walked down the hall to the sanctuary.

"No, I'm ok with sitting in the pews."

"Are you sure? I'd love to have you sit with me."

"Nah, I'm good. I don't want to draw any extra attention to myself."

"Ok, I understand," he kissed her lightly on the cheek and held the door for her to enter the sanctuary.

Just as he opened the door for her, there was Ms. All White, Sis. Yolanda, sitting in the pew with her arms folded and her face balled up because of Zoe's presence. Pastor Thad proceeded to take his place on the pulpit. Zoe sat on the front row like she did on Friday night. Sis. Yolanda just stared at her until it was uncomfortable. Zoe took her phone out, turned on her front facing camera and made sure she didn't have anything hanging out of her nose, or any lint stuck in her hair. There had to have been something wrong for Yolanda to stare at her the way she was. Zoe checked herself and everything looked fine. She realized that it was just a trick of the enemy, so she put her phone up, bowed her head and prayed until service started.

Pastor Thad began service with a congregational song. The praise team sat on the front pew to her right and they all had microphones. They joined in and helped him sing. He kept watching her even as he sung. She tried to divert her eyes from him, but he kept watching her. Pastor Thad had one of the ministers to do the prayer and the scripture. Just before he introduced Zoe to the congregation, the guest speaker walked in, knelt and prayed, greeted the pulpit constituents, and took his seat. The usher rushed to pass out programs. Three pictures were on it, Pastor Thad's, Prophet John Snipe and Elder Zoe Reed. She was shocked that he printed programs with her photo on it in such short notice. However, she felt special.

It was time for her to come up. The praise team seemed grateful to have a break. They all stood and sang along with her from the audience but without a microphone. Zoe sang two songs and felt as if she was having an outer body experience. When the songs were over, she took her seat. The people were all over the place in praise. The guest speaker was even kneeling on the floor in worship unto God. Pastor Thad took the microphone and tried to exalt the service but all she heard in the microphone was a muffled cry. The atmosphere was thick with the presence of God. Zoe lifted her hands and continued to worship the Lord as tears fell uncontrollably down her face.

Pastor Thad cleared his throat as the people began to take their seats and request Kleenex from the ushers. He began to exalt a little more. The guest speaker was back in his seat with his eyes closed and his iPad in hand. He was ready to preach. Pastor Thad thanked Elder Zoe publicly for being there and ushering them into the presence of the Lord in an even greater way. He then introduced Prophet Snipe. Prophet Snipe preached like a man on fire. Zoe stood up the majority of the sermon. He was quick and to the point but then he began prophesy. People were healed, set free and delivered. He passed the microphone back to Pastor Thad but just when he was about to take his seat, he took the microphone back.

"Pastor Thad, the Lord said to tell you, that he's heard your prayers."

Pastor Thad lifted his hands as a sign of receiving what was being said. However, Prophet Snipe stopped talking. He kept looking from the audience and back to Pastor Thad as he stood before him in the pulpit.

He finally tapped Pastor Thad's arm and said, "Follow me Man of God," he brought him before the altar and Pastor Thad's back was to the congregation. Prophet Snipe continued to speak, "You've been seeking the Lord for a wife."

Zoe's chest fell into her left big toe!

"God said to tell you, that your wait is over."

The musicians started rearing the music for a praise.

"The Lord said to tell you, Pastor Thad, that your wife is here!"

Sis. Yolanda stood up and began waving her hand and saying yes Lord. This was the first time Zoe saw her move the entire service. A few of the saints rolled their eyes at Yolanda as if they were annoyed by her.

Prophet Snipe took Pastor Thad's hand and pulled him next to Zoe. Zoe just knew she was going to pee in her clothes for real this time. He took Pastor Thad's hand and put Zoe's hand in his.

He continued. "Not many days hence, you two will be husband and wife. I'm not a lying Prophet. I don't know if you two are courting now, or if you even see each other that way but the Lord said you will be married!"

The church broke out into a crazy praise just like her church did during the morning service. Yolanda stopped praising though. Prophet Snipe was about to go back into the pulpit again, but he turned back to them. They were still holding hands, but both were in shock.

"The Lord also said to tell you to be aware of the witch. You have a witch among you but no weapon that is formed against you will work. Before I allow the witch to harm you, I will take them out!"

That was it. That was all the church needed to hear. Zoe and Pastor Thad danced like they had lost their mind. Prophet Snipe and the congregation joined them. Yolanda stood still with fire in her eyes. She leaned on the seat in the front of her with pure hatred on her face. She would not stand by and let some young chick come into her church and steal her man. She wanted Zoe dead!

Chapter 9

Who is Yolanda?

When the benediction was said, Zoe reached for her purse to leave. She was drying her eyes and collecting her water bottle when she heard Pastor Thad call her name from the pulpit. She turned around to see what he wanted. He put a finger up motioning for to her to wait. Yolanda watched them and angrily snatched her purse from the pew and stormed out of the side door. Zoe heard a few people giggling about her grand exit. A few of the women and men greeted her and said, "congrats in advance". They also commented on how prophetic the speaker was regarding the witch and reminded Zoe that everything would be alright.

Everyone wasn't so friendly though, a few of the lady's sashayed past her and rolled their eyes. Zoe just stood there and took it all in as she observed everyone. She knew that she and the Lord would have to talk further about the congregation. She knew how cruel church people could be. Saints are something different, but church people can cause your gangsta to reveal itself.

"Hey beautiful," Thad said as he embraced Zoe.

"Hey yourself." she blushed.

"Are you hungry? I'd love to take you to lunch. Besides, after that word, I think we have a lot to talk about. I hope he didn't scare you."

"No, not at all. Actually, the prophesy that I received this morning was very similar to what took place today."

"Really?" Thad said and put one of his hands in his pocket and rubbed his chin with the other as if in deep thought.

Zoe nodded a yes.

"Ok, well, would you mind us dropping your car off to your house and driving further into Summerville? I'd like to take you to this Hibachi spot there. The food is really good."

"Sure, that's fine," she said as they proceeded to leave the building.

They walked in unison, making small talk until they reached her car. He kissed her on the cheek and saw to it that she was secure. He went into his car and followed her home. Zoe wondered if he would always lock her seatbelt for her and chuckled to herself. When they arrived at her house, Zoe went in momentarily to check on Mr. Hundley. When she came back out, Thad seemed nervous.

She touched his arm and jolted him out of his thoughts. "Hey, are you ok?"

"No, not really."

"Why? What's wrong?"

"I just saw Yolanda pass your house. She lives downtown so she must have followed us. She gave me a very scary look, one that I've never seen before. Listen, I don't want to freak you out, but I want you to stay prayed up and watch your surroundings ok?"

"Ok, but am I missing something, Thad? At this point, you're making me nervous!"

He grabbed her hand and kissed the back of it with his eyes close. He pulled her into him and put one of his arms around her then lead her to his vehicle. "Let's get something to eat and we'll talk about it on the way. Is that alright?"

"Yeah, sure. That's fine," she said, with hesitancy.

He locked her in and made his way to the driver side. He was trying to shake the look that Yolanda gave him, but he knew that it meant war. He had to physically and spiritually prepare himself for whatever she had up her sleeves.

As he backed out the driveway, he glanced at Zoe. She looked really concerned. He didn't want to put a damper on their day, but they had to talk about Yolanda. He knew that she was the witch that the Prophet was speaking of. Many thought he was clueless regarding her, but he knew exactly who she was. He held her left hand and placed it on his leg as he drove. Zoe loved how affectionate he was with her. She was getting used to it.

"Zoe," Thad called her name interrupting thoughts.

She looked at him to let him know that he had her attention.

"Baby, Yolanda followed us here and that's not good."

"So, when did you start calling me baby and why would she follow us?"

"Well, you are my baby so I'm calling you that as of now! Yolanda would follow us because she's crazy and she's a witch. She's tried so many times to get to me, but it's never worked."

"Why would she try to get to you? I don't understand."

"She's obsessed with me, Zoe. She cooks and brings things to the church, she leaves things in my office for me to eat, and she's even popped up to my house with food. So, I've had to tell my armor bearers that no one is to allow her to bring anything to my office or even to the church for me to eat. I've come to the church and found weird things outside of my office door, things that I know were planted because of witchcraft. We would pray, put on gloves and clean it up. The first time she came to my house, I didn't let her in. I met her at the door and took what she cooked but I didn't eat it. She had a love note attached to it that I threw away. She came the second and last time with some deserts and I told her to never show up at my home again. I explained to her that I wasn't interested in being anything other than a Pastor to her. I also asked her to not cook or bake anything for me. I'm very particular about what I eat and who it comes from. She was upset when she left but it didn't stop her. She proceeded to buy me gifts, such as clothes, jewelry, cologne, shoes, etc. I rejected all of it."

Zoe just rested her head on the headrest and looked ahead as she took in what Thad was saying.

"When she realized that I wouldn't take anything from her, she took it a step further by tricking the secretary to call her up with a presentation. She told the secretary not to mention it because it was a surprise for me."

Zoe shifted in her seat to get a look at Thad's face. She couldn't believe what she was hearing.

He continued. "She made something for me. I don't even remember what it was at this point. It was a red dish. I'll never forget that it looked weird. She gave this long speech about her loving me as her Pastor and how she wanted to sow into my life. I was infuriated. Some of the congregation knows what she does so they were just as angry as I was. However, she didn't stop there, she opened the dish and took out a fork and asked me to taste it in the front of the congregation."

"Wait, what? Weren't you all still technically having service?"

"Yep, we sure were. When I said no, she asked two or three more times and I abruptly told the armor bearer to take her dish from her. I didn't have to tell them to dispose of it. They already knew that. I remember it having a very foul smell. I don't know what she put in it, but I knew that it was something to either control me or kill me."

"Yikes! That's crazy, Thad!"

"Yes, it is crazy but heck, she's crazy!"

They both laughed as he turned into the parking lot of the restaurant. He parked and helped her out of the car. They went into the restaurant and were quickly seated at a table for two. Zoe ordered mango tea and a broiled scallop dinner with fried green tomatoes. He ordered the same. The server brought them cornbread while they waited on their food to arrive. They continued with small talk regarding Yolanda and other things too.

"Zoe, I told you all of this because Yolanda really believes that we are to be married. We've never dated. I've never seen her that way and I've never given her any inclination that we'd be more than Pastor and parishioner. She's conjured this stuff up all on her own. In addition to how crazy she is, she's dangerous. Her family is rooted in witchcraft. That's what they're known for. I just want you to be aware. Ok?"

"Ok Thad, I hear you."

Just then, their food arrived, and it looked divine. They said their grace and proceeded to eat.

"Now, tell me about this prophecy that you received today."

"It was pretty simple but a big deal at the same time. He basically said that I was about to be married and that I wouldn't be single much longer," she giggled and covered her mouth with her napkin. "The church broke out into a dance just like yours did this afternoon. It was definitely confirmation of things that I've been in prayer about."

Thad watched her lips as she spoke. She was such a beautiful woman. He would marry her that day if he thought she'd say yes. He was feeling way more for her than what he was revealing. The truth is, he had already fallen in love with her. Her worship, her beauty, her ambition, it all did something to him. He loved every bit of it.

"Wow! Our God is awesome, isn't he?"

"Yes, he certainly is."

"Ok, now how do you feel about what Prophet Snipe said about you and me? Has the Lord confirmed that in your spirit?"

"Honestly, I've been in prayer regarding you, but I wasn't sure until today. Sometimes, we get so caught up in what we want that our ears either deafen to where we can't hear the Holy Spirit, or we enter a fantastical world where we hear what we want. It's at those times that I need the Lord to send a prophet. So, I'm ok with what he said."

Thad had a look on his face that Zoe couldn't discern. He looked happy and freaked out at the same time.

"I definitely believe it was God, Zoe. I've been by myself for so long that sometimes the routine becomes comfortable. However, I know that it's time for me to move on with my life. I didn't realize that until I met you. I know it's only been a few days, but I feel like I've known you forever. I believe this is God. I'm older now and it doesn't take me long to figure out what I want. I just don't want to be overbearing with you. I don't want to make you feel rushed."

"I don't feel like you're rushing me, Thad. I don't feel that way at all."

"Yeah right!"

"I'm serious. I know that it's literally been a few days but, I like our pace. I feel like this is it."

"Alright, so if I got down on one knee right now, in this restaurant, and asked you to marry me, would you say yes?"

"I just might. You never know," Zoe said daringly.

Thad got up from his seat and got down on one knee. Zoe's breathe caught in her chest and she thought she would die right there. She exhaled deeply and looked so nervous that Thad burst into laughter as he sat back in his chair.

He thought for a moment and said, "See, I knew you weren't serious. We just met. You're not ready to marry and old guy like me," he looked at his plate and cut his scallop in half.

"First of all, you're not old."

"I'm older than you!"

"Ok, and so what? I find you very attractive, Thad. You just scared me because I wasn't expecting you to do that," she started laughing nervously as she relived the moment in her mind. She shifted her head to the side and looked at him. She reached over the table and took his hand into hers. "Although you almost gave me a heart attack, I'm ninety-five percent sure that I would've said yes."

Their dinner was filled with laughter and moments of intimate words. Yolanda wasn't spoken of for the rest of the meal, but she sat on the back of their minds.

Chapter 10

Witchcraft planted...

The drive home came too fast. Neither of them wanted the date to end. She was off the next day anyway, being that it was Monday, and so was he. When they pulled into her driveway, both of their eyes scanned the outside of the house without mentioning it to the other. Thad opened her door and walked her to the front door of her house instead of entering through the garage like she normally does. As soon as they got near the porch, they both noticed black seeds lining the step. They were laid neatly up against the step. Thad immediately reached for Zoe's hand and squeezed it. They both knew that Yolanda had planted it. Thad immediately went into a prayer and quoted Isaiah 54:17.

"Go and get your broom, dustpan and a grocery bag, please. I'll wait here."

Zoe quickly stepped over the black seeds, opened her door, gathered the items and returned to Thad. Thad swept the seeds into the dustpan and dumped them into the grocery bag. She brought two, so he wrapped the end of the broom in the second grocery bag and threw it all into his trunk.

"I'll purchase another broom for you."

"You don't have to do that. I can take care of that."

He noticed that Zoe was still standing at the front door. Her arms were folded, and she looked worried. His protective stance took over and before he knew it, he was holding her and kissing her forehead. No words were spoken. They didn't need to be.

"Would you like to come in for a while? I was thinking maybe we could watch a movie."

"I'd love to. I have a change of clothes in my car. Would you mind if I changed while I'm here?"

"Sure you can. I'll see you on the inside. As a matter of fact, you can park in the garage next to my car. Now that we have a stalker, that might be best."

Thad agreed and proceeded to park in the garage. He grabbed his duffel bag of clothes and entered the house through the garage door. Zoe showed him to the guest bedroom and bathroom. She laid out fresh towels and soap in case he wanted to shower. Thad smiled at how thoughtful she was and at the cleanliness of her home. It felt like he was at a five-star hotel. He quickly took advantage of the shower and came out in a V-neck t-shirt with some Nike sweatpants and Nike slippers. He was happy to rid himself of his church attire. He cleaned up behind himself, put his dirty clothes into the car and waited for Zoe in the living room. As soon as Mr. Hundley saw him, he came and jumped on his lap. Thad welcomed him with a few strokes on his back.

After Zoe showered, she came down in a peak-a-boo, red, shoulder dress and her house slippers. She smiled as she saw Thad and her dog bonding. "Well, don't you look refreshed!"

"Thanks, and you're looking fine as always in that red dress!"

She blushed and said, "Thank you! So, what movie would you like to watch?" She grabbed a blanket and the remote, then cuddled up next to him and Mr. Hundley. Her home was always cold because she kept the air conditioner on sixty-eight degrees.

Thad pulled on the blanket so they could share it. She searched through the Netflix line up and they both agreed to watch the movie called, *Something New,* starring one of her favorite actresses, Sanaa Lathan. Mr. Hundley left them and got into his bed on the floor. Thad and Zoe scooted closer and she rested her head on his shoulder as they watched the movie.

The entire time, Thad stole kisses from her forehead, her cheeks, her ear and finally her mouth. Eventually, the movie was watching them. The blanket was thrown to the floor and Thad's upper body completely covered Zoe's! The sound of Zoe moaning and Thad groaning startled Mr. Hundley and he awoke barking at them. They jumped, looked and him and giggled a little.

Realization set in for them both and they said in unison, "It's getting late."

They fell into laughter at their realization that with a few more minutes of passion and they'd both be on the altar repenting. Thad squeezed Zoe's hand, stood up and pulled her with him. He pecked her on the lips before heading towards the garage to leave.

"I meant to tell you that my daughters will be here this weekend. I'd love for you to meet them."

"Your-your daughters?" Zoe stuttered.

"Yes!" He took both of Zoe's hands into his and looked into her eyes. "I believe the prophet, Zoe. I also believe that I've personally heard God concerning you. I want you to meet my daughters. I don't want to waste any time with you. Are you ok with that?"

"Umm, yes, I think so. I'm just nervous."

"For what? They're going to love you!" He planted one more kiss on her cheek and opened his car door to leave. Her lips were a bit swollen from him kissing her earlier. He came to her once more and stole another kiss. Without realizing it, he'd pinned her to his vehicle while he kissed her. He lost all sense of consciousness as his lower body moved against her on its own accord. Zoe felt way more than she expected and began to push him away. Thad only tightened his grip. Zoe pinched him on his upper arm and he removed his grip and his lips. He backed away while rubbing him arm where she pinched him.

"What was that for? You pinch like the old church mothers!" He was still rubbing the spot as he said it.

"That's for you being fresh Sir!"

Thad laughed a little but still rubbed his arm. "I'll call you as soon as I get home." He leaned in for another kiss, but Zoe gave him her cheek.

They both laughed at her act of sarcasm and Thad got into his car to leave.

ZOE OPENED THE GARAGE DOOR AND WATCHED HIM EXIT BEFORE CLOSING IT AGAIN.

Chapter 11

Meeting Ava and Autumn

The weekend arrived faster than Zoe expected. She could barely eat or sleep all week in anticipation of meeting Thad's daughters. Thad had arranged for them to have lunch at Charlie's Roadhouse at 2:00pm on Saturday. This gave Zoe enough time to see her clients, clean the salon and prepare for their lunch. She wore a pair of ripped jeans and a turquoise blouse with one shoulder out. Her curls were fabulous, and she wore minimal lipstick. She needed some stability on her feet, so she settled for a pair of black Michael Kors wedges verses her normal three to four-inch heels. She arrived at the restaurant shortly after two and the hostess escorted her to the booth. Thad and his daughters were already seated and laughing like old friends. She noticed in those few seconds that their bond was unbreakable. She inwardly prayed that they liked her. Thad noticed her approaching and his eyes lit up like a Christmas tree. He stood to greet her and kissed her cheek.

"You look gorgeous, babe."

"Thanks, Thad," Zoe blushed.

"Ava, Autumn, I'd like you to meet the lady in my life, Zoe Reed."

They both said hello in unison and Zoe responded with hello while shaking their hands.

Thad stepped aside for Zoe to slide into the booth and he sat next to her. Ava and Autumn sat across from them. Zoe felt like every butterfly in the world was captured and placed in her belly. Thad's hand immediately landed on her thigh. He unconsciously stroked the bare skin that lied beneath her ripped jeans. Zoe, on the other hand was very aware!

"So, how was traffic on the way here from Charlotte?" Zoe asked to make small talk to ignore the stir that Thad was causing under the table.

"It was ok," Autumn offered but Ava rolled her eyes and looked at the menu. "We left Charlotte at approximately ten. We got some snacks and hit the road. There wasn't a lot of traffic on the road at all."

Before Zoe could respond Ava chimed in. "So, exactly how old are you, Zoe?"

"Ava, that's uncouth of you," Thad interjected.

"I mean, she looks like she's our age, so I'm just wondering that's all," Ava said as she shrugged her shoulders pretending to study the menu.

"Wow, well, your Dad tells me that you and your sister are twenty-eight and twenty-six, if I'm not mistaken. I'm actually thirty-nine so thanks for the compliment," Zoe sat back in her seat and her stance said that she was up for the challenge that Ava was presenting.

Autumn yanked Zoe out of her thoughts by saying, "What? There's no way that you're thirty-nine! You look so young! I mean, not that you're old but girl I need to know what cream you're using. You look good."

Everyone at the table chuckled except Ava. She was certainly in her feelings about Thad seeing Zoe.

"So, Dad will we be seeing Sister Yolanda today? I was hoping she'd stop by with some sweet potato pie. She makes the best pie," said Ava. She smirked and glanced back at her menu.

Zoe shifted in her seat with a look of confusion on her face. Ava spoke of Yolanda as if her presence was welcomed, when Thad described their affiliation as something completely different.

"Ava you know we don't deal with Yolanda like that." Autumn quickly added before Thad had a chance too. "You're the only one who deals with that crazy chick!"

Zoe breathed relief at the confirmation of Thad's truth. Thad shook his head from side to side, "Ava, you're grown, and I can't tell you what to do. However, I've warned you before about dealing with her. She's a dangerous woman. You don't need to take anything from her, especially food!"

"Daddy, you know me and Sis. Yolanda have always been cool. I just think she's right for you," she gave Zoe a very devious look. "She is closer to your age, she cooks, cleans, she's faithful to the ministry and I know that she'll take care of you. That's all I'm saying."

"Ava, you're being downright rude. I don't expect you to treat my guest this way. You need to apologize now!"

Zoe was startled by the stern way Thad spoke to Ava but appreciated him defending her.

"Sorry, Zoe, but I'm not fake and I'm just not feeling this."

Zoe looked between Thad and his daughters. Thad looked embarrassed. Autumn looked apologetic and Ava looked like she had won a battle that Zoe wasn't aware that she was a part of.

Zoe looked at Thad and whispered, "Maybe I should go."

He put his arm around her shoulder. "No, you don't have to go anywhere."

"Ava, let me see you outside please," he threw his cloth napkin on the table and headed for the door without waiting to see if Ava was coming or not.

Autumn's eyes stretched and she looked like a little girl who knew her big sister was in big trouble. Ava placed her menu on the table and headed for the door behind Thad. She made sure to look Zoe in the eyes to express her depth of dislike for her before leaving the table. Zoe held her gaze of being unmoved and that she would meet her in the war room!

Ava saw her father outside and approached him. "Yes, Daddy?"

"Ava, how dare you be so rude to Zoe! You don't know her or anything about her! This isn't how I raised you. What's gotten into you? Why are you behaving this way?" He asked the questions so fast that Ava didn't have a chance to answer any of them. "Listen, I know you miss your mother, but I'm still alive and I'm still young. I need companionship. You and your sister are off in Charlotte living your lives and I don't interfere with it. Zoe makes me happy. Her age is not a factor to me, Ava. She's made me feel things over the past few weeks that I haven't felt in years. I need you to be ok with this. The way you're treating her hurts me because she doesn't deserve that."

"Dad, that chick is just out for your money. She knows you have a big house, a nice car and you're a Pastor. She's trying to get a check. She just met you! There's no way you two can be in love."

"We are, Ava. She's not trying to get a check from me. She owns a very nice house in Summerville, she owns a hair salon and she's a preacher too."

"Yeah and how many children does she have? I know she has children! As big as she is, she's got to have pushed out at least two or three nappy heads by now!"

"Why are you being rude and making these assumptions? First, I love her size and her shape. In case you forgot, your Mother was a large woman. It's very disrespectful for you to speak of her or any other woman that way!"

"Sorry, Daddy."

"She doesn't have any children. She's never been married. Her father is a Pastor and she's a very sweet person. All I'm asking is that you give her a chance. Would you do that for me, please?"

Ava didn't want to comply, but she said, "Yes, Daddy. I'll give her a chance," her mouth said yes but her heart devised a wicked plan.

What her Dad and Autumn didn't know was that she and Yolanda became friends over the years. Yolanda purposefully got close to Autumn to keep up with Thad's personal life. She would cry on the phone with her about how much she loved Thad. She even lied to Ava about conversations between her and Thad that never took place. She fantasied about dates between the two of them. However, although she shared these dates with Ava as though they were real, she also convinced her to never mention it to Thad or he would break up with her because he's so private. Ava wanted to mention Yolanda to her Dad, but she knew she couldn't. She was beginning to feel confused about why Thad would hide his relationship with Yolanda but would put Zoe on display. Was it because Zoe was younger and made him look good? She was going to find out the truth. She would be on her best behavior, for now. Ava and Thad arrived back at the table smiling and making small talk. She had to convince her Father that all was well. She sat across from Zoe once again.

"Zoe, I apologize for how I behaved earlier. I just miss my mom and I want my Dad to be happy, that's all."

"I accept your apology. I'm not trying to replace anyone. I just love your Father," she stopped talking to look at him. He squeezed her hand under the table. Her heart seemed to have stopped beating momentarily because she said that she loved him. "I just want to make him happy." she looked at him again.

"I love you too, Zoe," They continued to look into each other's eyes as if no one else was in the room.

Autumn interrupted their moment when she clasped her hands together and said, "Oh that is so sweet! Oh my geez, Daddy's got a girlfriend!"

Ava forced a smile but didn't say anything. She continued to pretend to read the menu. She was relieved that the server came and took their orders. The food arrived and they made small talk. Autumn and Zoe held the conversation while Thad observed their interaction. Ava just sat quietly. When dinner was over, Thad walked Zoe to her car.

"So, you love me huh?"

"Yeah, I guess," she laughed and shrugged her shoulders.

"Seriously, do you really love me?"

"Yes, Mr. Thad Wescott, I really do love you," she said and wrapped her arms around his waist.

He kissed her nose and said, "I love you, too."

Ava beeped the car horn because she was disgusted with their public display of affection. He forgot that they were parked near each other and they could see them.

He chuckled against Zoe's forehead and kissed her there. "I'll call you later, ok?"

"Ok." Zoe got into the car and he reached in to put on her seatbelt. While backing out of her car. He pecked her on the lips.

"Will you stop by the church tomorrow?"

"Yes, if we get out early enough."

"Ok. I'll call you later this evening," he tapped the hood of her car and she pulled away from the parking space to leave the restaurant. She had mixed feelings. She was shocked that she stated to him that she loved him and in the front of his daughters. However, she was hurt that Ava did not approve of their relationship. She was happy that Autumn was trying to get to know her. Family was important to her. She hoped that their love would be enough to see them through this.

Chapter 12

Late Night Talk...

At almost nine o'clock Thad called Zoe. She answered the phone while she was laying on her couch, with Mr. Hundley on her lap, watching the Lifetime channel. They made small talk for a while and then they glided into the subject that they both were trying to avoid.

"So, Ava hates me, huh?"

"No, she doesn't hate you. She's just upset because she really doesn't want to see me with another woman if it's not her Mother. She would tolerate me being with Yolanda but that would never happen! Just give her some time. Now, Autumn fell in love with you. Either way, what my daughters feel matters, but in this case, it doesn't. They have their lives and I have mine. They are young and vibrant. I'm just trying to be happy at this point. God gave us his approval and confirmation on today. That's all I need! To top it off, you told me that you love me. The Lord knows I love you, so I'm all smiles right now."

Zoe smiled at his comment but didn't say anything.

"So, do you believe me when I say that I love you, Zoe?

"Yeah, I believe you. I can't believe that we're having these feelings so soon but it's undeniably true. I mean, people have met, married within less than one week and stayed married. If it happened then, I'm sure that it could happen now."

"You're absolutely right. When I got on my knees you seemed a little nervous though."

"Well, I was nervous! She laughed a little. I wasn't expecting you to do that!"

"I guess it's safe to say that you're not ready to marry me at this very moment."

"Not at this very moment. One of your daughters wants me to disappear and the other is thrilled about me. Then there's the situation with Yolanda. There just seems to be things that we have to work on."

"I agree with you, if those are your concerns. However, they are not any of my concerns. I know what God is saying and I know how I feel. There's nothing that anyone can say or do to change that."

"Ok, let's turn the table for a moment, Thad."

"Ok. Let's do it."

"So, if I said I was ready to marry you now, despite how Ava feels, you would still marry me right now Thad?"

"I'd say let's do it tomorrow at church!"

Zoe leaned over in laughter.

"What's funny? I'm serious. Matter of fact, what size do you wear in rings?"

"Thad, I'm not disclosing that information to you," she said while still slightly giggling and wiping tears from her eyes.

"Why not? I need to know so your ring can be properly sized."

"You don't even know what type of ring I would want!"

"Let me guess…white gold, square shaped diamond, not too bulky, simple but elegant. I'd think you'd like a princess styled ring to sum it all up."

Zoe stopped smiling and was glad that he couldn't see her face because he was on point with his accuracy.

"Hello, is my soon to be fiancé home?" Thad quipped.

"Yeah, I'm here," she said trying to sound as if he was wrong.

"Ok, so don't keep me guessing. Did I peg you right? Is that what you would want?"

"Yes, you're right, Thad. Geesh!"

This time Thad had the pleasure of laughing, "Ok now tell me what size you wear in rings."

"Nope."

"What? Why not?"

"Because I don't want to," she said playfully.

"Zoe, don't make me come over there!"

"Whatever! Ain't nobody scared of you!"

"Alright, let's see how unafraid you are on our wedding night! You're talking all this trash now."

"Yep! I'll be talking trash then too!"

"Alright, well as us old folk say, 'I'm going to show you better than I can tell you'."

Zoe was really laughing now but Thad wasn't at all.

"Hello?"

"I'm here."

"Why are you quiet?"

"Because you think I'm joking. Don't let my age fool you. I've already envisioned what I'm going to do to you. Just remember that the marriage bed is undefiled! You were pushing me off of you earlier and not the other way around, remember. You didn't know how to act when I had you pinned to my car."

Zoe had tears rolling down her face because she couldn't believe he was talking to her like that. It was hilarious to her. Mr. Hundley was peeking at her through heavy eyelids because she was waking him up with all of the noise.

"Ok, Pastor Thad, I think we need to change the subject."

"Why did you have to go there? I've got your Pastor Thad! Yeah, we need to hurry up and get married. What size do you wear in rings, Zoe?"

While still laughing at his persistence and his frustration, she told him a size six and a half.

"Wow you have tiny fingers. We call them piano fingers."

"Yes, I've heard that before."

"Thank you for telling me. Now I can get to work."

"Seriously Thad, how soon are you looking at being married?"

"I'd like us to be married as soon as possible but no more than a year. I can't wait that long. I need you to be my wife now."

"Is this just a sexual thing, Thad? Is that where your anxiousness is coming from?"

"No, that's a part of it but I want to have you here with me. I'm not twenty anymore. I want to wake up to you every morning and hold you while you sleep at night. I want to travel with you and do things with you without feeling convicted. It's been a long time since I've been this happy. I just want it full-time."

"I understand. Well, it's getting late. It's already after eleven o'clock. I can't believe we've been on the phone this long. I need to go to bed!"

"Come on. It's still early," Thad teased.

"No sir, it is not! I'm turning off this TV right now and going upstairs to my bed."

"Ok. Give me ten minutes. I'm on the way."

"You are too silly, Thad. You're not going anywhere but to bed yourself!"

"Yeah, you're right. Ava and Autumn should be back soon. They went to visit a few of their old friends. I do have to wrap up my sermon for tomorrow. You're still coming right?"

"Yes, if we get out at a reasonable time."

"Alright. I understand."

"I'm going to go and get myself together for real. If you don't make it to church, come by my house please. Ava and Autumn are going back home tomorrow. I'd like for you to be here with me to see them off."

"Ok, I'll do that."

"I love you, Zoe."

She blushed so hard she thought her cheeks would be stuck.

"I love you too, Thad."

They both said goodnight. Zoe ensured that her doors were locked and went to bed. Thad went online to complete his sermon. Afterwards, however, he shopped for a size six and a half ring. He found two or three that he liked, emailed them to himself and went to bed. Life was getting better by the minute.

Chapter 13

I Wasn't Ready...

Sunday's service was amazing. Zoe's Elect lady preached, and the church was on fire with the power of the Holy Ghost. Zoe felt like she was walking on clouds by the time service was over. She greeted everyone and decided to go to lunch with her parents. Thad could wait to see her after lunch. Besides, she was famished after all the dancing, hollering and running she had done.

They went to a soul food buffet of course. A few of the other ministers and their families joined them. Zoe's best friend, Tyler, came along as well. Zoe had called her that morning before church to update her on Thad's daughter and the incident with Yolanda. Tyler reminded her that she still had some Vaseline, and a pair of tennis shoes in her car. Zoe laughed but appreciated her friend's willingness to fight for her. While laughing and enjoying their lunch, Thad called. Zoe excused herself from the table to take the call.

"Hi there."

"Hey, I was hoping you'd come by the church today."

"Yeah, I decided to have lunch with my parents. I haven't done that in a while."

"I completely understand. I was calling to see if you wanted to meet my daughters and I for lunch since they'll be heading to Charlotte right afterwards.

However, since you're at lunch now, maybe you can meet us at the airport?"

Zoe proceeded to the buffet to prepare another plate when she spotted Thad walking in the door with his daughters.

"Then again, it looks like we'll be having lunch together after all."

Thad spotted Zoe as well and rushed over to embrace her. Autumn was all smiles and hugged Zoe. Ava embraced her, but it was very cold. They made small talk for a moment until the hostess asked them how many people would be at their table. Zoe asked the hostess to give them a minute and she pulled Thad aside.

"My parents are here. I wasn't prepared for you to meet them today and your daughters. My legs are shaking right now. Is that something you're ready for?"

"Absolutely, lead the way! Ava, Autumn, Zoe's family is here. Let's go and say hello."

Zoe stood there for a moment with her mouth agape. She was in shock and unable to move.

"Zoe, are you going to show us to your parent's table?"

"Uh yeah, sure. Let's go."

Zoe made her way over to the table and stood next to her parents. She felt like she was twelve years old and introducing her crush to her father, especially.

"Mom, Dad, this is my friend, Pastor Thad Wescott and his daughters, Ava and Autumn. Thad, Ava and Autumn, these are my parents, Pastor and Lady Reed."

They greeted each other, and Zoe's mom kept giving her the eye as if she knew that they were more than friends. Zoe had mentioned him a few times, but she was not ready for this gathering. Just then Zoe's dad zapped her out of her thoughts by offering Thad and his daughters to join them.

Without consulting his daughters, he asked, "Zoe is that ok with you?"

The look in Thad's eye when he addressed Zoe told Zoe's dad all that he needed to know. This is the mysterious guy that Zoe has been hinting to her mother about. They didn't know he was that much older than her and with adult children. Yet, her father felt a peace about it.

"Y-yes that's fine."

The other ministers and their families decided to leave to make space for Thad and his daughters at the table. They'd been at the restaurant for almost two hours, so it was time to go. He sat right next to Zoe. The server came over and took their drink orders. Zoe's appetite had left because she was so nervous.

Thad and his daughters excused themselves to make their plates. As soon as they left. Tyler fell over in laughter and her parents seemed to ask one hundred questions in a matter of seconds. They wanted to know if they were officially dating, how old was he, how old were his daughters, is this serious, etc.

Zoe held up her hands and said, "It's a long story but Thad is 51 and his daughters are in their mid-twenties. They live in Charlotte. Thad pastors a church in downtown Charleston and yes, we are officially dating. They're coming back to the table so y'all please behave."

Zoe's dad sat back in his chair and just observed the two of them. He was only sixty- two. He couldn't understand why his daughter would be interested in a man who was so much older than her. He stirred his fork along his plate, but the food never made it back to his mouth. They all talked among themselves. Tyler and Zoe's mom questioned Pastor Thad about him and Zoe. He revealed his intentions. He was going to make Zoe his wife. Her mom was ecstatic. Tyler and Autumn were ready to go and pick out the dress. However, Ava and Zoe's dad were staring into space. They were not happy about the news they'd just heard.

Zoe paid attention to it all and so did Thad. In order to further his point, he grabbed Zoe's hand and squeezed it underneath the table. They glanced at each other and he gave her a look of comfort. She smiled and resumed conversation with everyone at the table. An hour later, it was time for them to leave. Ava and Autumn needed to head back to Charlotte.

Zoe said goodbye to her parents. Her dad asked her to call him when she got some time and she agreed to. She was nervous though because her parent's approval meant everything to her. Her mom was on board, so she'd call her mom first.

Zoe walked over to Thad and his daughters as they prepared to leave.

"Are you following us to my house?" Thad asked. They needed to load their bags into the car.

"Dad, I'm sure Zoe's tired from having such a long day. Maybe she should go home and rest for the day. We're ok with saying our goodbyes now," Ava interjected.

Thad frowned at Ava and then turned back to Zoe. "Would you follow me, please?"

Zoe made eye contact with the three of them, but Thad's approval was all she needed.

"Sure, I can follow you."

He kissed her on the cheek. He saw to it that his daughters were in their car and that she was as well. He got into his vehicle and proceeded to head to his house with his daughters and Zoe in tow.

While riding there, Zoe's dad called her before she had the chance to call him. She could hear her mother in the background pleading with him to leave it alone before Zoe could say hello. He had her on speaker phone.

"Hello," She answered reluctantly.

"Zoe, what are you doing with this man? You're not that much older than his daughters!"

"Dad, I'm headed to Thad's house with them right now. I can't talk long but I have a question for you."

"Alright, what is it?"

"Do you remember the prophecy from just a few days ago about me getting married?"

He sighed with regret. "Yes, I do."

"Would you believe that I went to Thad's church that same day and we received the same prophecy, together?"

"Wow!" Her mother chimed in in the background.

Her Dad was astounded.

"Dad, I know his age is an issue for you. Honestly, I'm still wrapping my head around it. However, we do love each other even though we've just met. He's not using me for anything. He has his own house, vehicles, money, etc. His ex-wife died over twenty years ago. His ministry is huge, and marriage is in our future. It's probably going to happen soon. Well it is going to happen as soon as the prophecy stated. He's not trying to sleep with me. He's the perfect gentleman and I do love him, Daddy."

Her mom was clutching her pearls at hearing the news. Zoe hadn't told her all the details before. She only said that she met someone, and things were getting serious.

"Ok, baby girl. If you're happy then that's all that matters. I just don't want you to get hurt. One of his daughters doesn't seem so happy about you two."

"I know, but it's ok. Thad has made it clear to them that he loves them, but he has to live his life as well."

"Ok, just know that I'm here for you. I don't want you to rush into anything. Please be prayerful, ok, Zoe?"

"Ok, Daddy."

"I love you girl!"

Zoe laughed. "I love you too, Daddy."

"Mommy loves you three!"

Zoe laughed harder at her mom's sweetness. "I love you four Mommy."

They said their goodbyes and Zoe exhaled. She was amazed at how smooth that went over. She thought it would be worst. Her parents are very protective of her and her siblings. God's hands were certainly in this!

Zoe arrived at Thad's home. Thad opened the car doors for his daughters, then went over to Zoe's car to open her door. Just as Zoe exited her vehicle, Ava approached her. Zoe noticed that Autumn gave Ava a look that said, *do the right thing*.

"Zoe can we chat for a second?"

Zoe took a deep breath and said, "Sure."

"Look, I'm not jumping up and down with joy about you and my Dad. However, I see that he is crazy about you. I don't like the fact that you're much younger than him but it's not my business. Autumn came down on me pretty hard in the car about my attitude towards you. I know that God's not happy about it either. Just please do me one favor?"

"Ok, what is it.?"

"If you're not serious about him, please leave him alone. It took him a long time to get over the death of our Mother. Yolanda has been after him for years and she's pretty, but he wouldn't even consider it. You come along, and I feel like I've never seen this side of him before."

"Ava, I appreciate your apology. Nevertheless, I need you to know that there is nothing fake about me. I'm not a liar. What you see is what you get. I'm here with your Dad because I want to be. His age is an issue for me as well. Did you ever consider that? I don't need his money. I have my own. I don't need his house. I have my own. I don't need his ministry. I have my own with my parents. I'm here because your Father has captured my heart. I've fallen in love with him. Am I scared? Absolutely! But I've been with men my age and it didn't work. I'll tell you like I just told my father, on the way over here, we both got the same prophecy a few days ago about us being married. I'm thirty-nine. I'm not twenty-two anymore. In this season, and those to come, I have no choice but to trust God. The way your father makes me feel, no other man has made me feel this way."

"Alright, alright, I don't want to hear all of that. It's too much info!"

"No, no, I'm not talking about sexually. We are not partaking in that until marriage. I just want you to know that what I feel for your dad is real."

Ava took a deep breath and said, "I believe you. Can I give you a real hug?"

They both laughed a little and embraced. When they pulled apart. Thad and Autumn were standing on the doorstep watching them with smiles plastered on their faces.

"I am sorry for how I treated you, Zoe. I hope you can forgive me."

"I already have!"

Thad and Autumn walked towards them and Autumn said, "Well alright, there is a God!"

They said their goodbyes and Zoe went inside with Thad. When they got inside. He locked the door and pulled her into him for an embrace. As they pulled away, no words were spoken. Instead, Thad kissed Zoe as if he'd never kissed her before. It was a long, slow, tender and passionate kiss. This kiss said I love you and I'm ready to move forward.

When the kiss was over, Zoe staggered a little. "Um, maybe I should go home. I don't think it's safe for me to be here after that kiss," Zoe joked.

Thad still didn't respond. He gathered her face into her hands and kissed her again. This time, her back was against the wall. Her hands were free, yet she didn't know where to put them. She kept them at her sides. She didn't know what was happening. This kiss had nothing to do with sex. He was speaking to her through this kiss. He was trying to tell her something. The kiss ended but he kept his hands on either side of her face. He said nothing. He just stared into her eyes.

Zoe cleared her throat. "Thad, what is it? What's wrong? Why are you looking at me like that?"

"Because the love that I feel for you is overwhelming. The two most important people to me, other than you, just left. Even their opinions couldn't move me. I'm convinced that you are the woman the Lord has set aside for me. I have to make you my wife and soon."

Zoe swallowed hard and whispered, "ok."

Thad released her and led her into the kitchen. "The girls baked a cake on last night. Would you like to try some?" He asked while cutting himself a slice.

"After all the food I've just eaten, I couldn't eat another bite. I should be eating a salad anyway."

"Why do you say that?"

"Whatever, I'm not petite like your daughters."

Thad shook his head and licked the icing from his fork while watching Zoe.

"What's that look for?"

"Because I can't wait to marry you so that I can show you how much I love each and every inch of your body. You don't need to lose a pound!"

Zoe blushed but didn't respond. Thad walked around the island where she was sitting and dipped his forefinger into her mouth before she could resist. She jumped because she wasn't expecting it but relaxed at the taste of icing that covered the tip of his finger.

He stood there and watched her reaction, primarily her lips as she enjoyed the taste of the chocolate delight. She savored the taste and all he could think of was savoring her.

Chapter 14

I'll Hang Your Lights for You!

Months went by and the hustle and bustle of the holidays were upon them. Zoe loved Christmas so every year she put her decorations up on the Sunday prior to Thanksgiving. She always prepared Thanksgiving dinner at her house and her family and friends came over. She invited Thad and his daughters over for the holiday. They accepted her invitation and she was ecstatic. Just as she was setting her Christmas elves decorations around the house. Her doorbell rang. It was Thad.

"What a pleasant surprise!" She greeted him with a warm hug and a peck on the lips. Mr. Hundley made a mad dash for him and jumped for Thad to greet him. "What brings you by?"

"I tried calling you, but your phone just rang so I figured I'd would stop by. I hope that's ok."

"Yeah, it's perfectly fine."

"Did you enjoy service today?"

"Yes, you did a great job with the message as you always do!"

"Thanks. I'm going to have to book you to come and preach soon."

"Ok, sounds like a plan."

Zoe was so excited about Thad coming over that she'd forgotten about her attire. She was wearing a tank job with a pair of leggings and Christmas socks. She wasn't wearing any makeup and she had a scarf on to keep her edges laid. She noticed that his eyes roamed her body and she looked down at herself to see what was wrong.

"Oh em Geez, please excuse my attire! I usually wear things like this to clean or whatever. Give me a second to change, please."

He grabbed her wrist just as she was walking by to head upstairs. "Please don't. You look fine." He slightly touched her chin to reaffirm his words.

"Ok, so you were calling. What's up?"

"Well, I know you're having dinner here. I wanted to see if I could help. Looks like you have Christmas décor to put up outside and inside."

"Yeah, but I have my ladder so I can put that stuff up in no time."

"Let me help you. If we're married, you're not going to be doing this alone."

He walked closer to the door and picked up some lights that were lying on the floor.

"Thad you really don't have to do that."

"Let me help you, please."

"Ok, if you insist."

"I do insist! Can I start on these lights?"

"Yes, that's fine. Let's go into the garage to gather more tools."

Thad climbed the ladder to hang her lights. The nails were still in place from the previous years. He secured them, tested the lights to make sure they worked and proceeded to his next project. He found some trimmers in her garage and trimmed her hedges. He raked the leaves that were scattered and cleaned whatever he could on the outside. When he came in almost two hours later, he found her struggling to put the star on the tree. He chuckled, came up behind her, took the star from her hand and placed it on the tree.

"Why are you working harder than you have to?" He wrapped his arms around her waist and kissed her right shoulder.

She reached up and touched the back of his head as he held her. She rubbed it a little, loving that he sometimes wore it bald. "Because that's what I'm used to Thad," she pulled away from his embrace. "I've been by myself for a long time. I'm used to getting it done and not depending on other people."

"Well, I'm about to change all of that. Now, I've worked hard today, and you have this kitchen smelling right! Can you feed me please?"

Zoe giggled. "Sure, I'll fix you a plate."

She had cooked some beef barbecue ribs with sweet potato and steamed cabbage. Thad ate while she cleared her living room of storage boxes that she had kept her Christmas items in. They talked about what the holidays meant to them and family traditions. He expressed how excited he was to be a part of her life and that she invited him and his daughters over for Thanksgiving.

"Zoe."

"Yes, Sir?"

"Don't think that I didn't notice that you went and put on a big t-shirt. Why did you do that?"

"Because I was uncomfortable with you seeing me in my tank top."

"Why? Did you think I would try you?"

"No. Well yeah, but no. I'm just not comfortable with other people seeing me in things like that. I only wear it around the house. Like I said, I'm not a petite woman. I don't want you seeing all of my flaws!"

Thad left where he was sitting, at the island, and walked into the living room where she was cleaning. He stopped her by pulling her towards him.

"What flaws?"

"Thad, really? Let's not do this."

"Let's not do what? What flaws?"

"So, you're telling me that you don't see all of these rolls. My stomach protrudes and I've never been pregnant. My hips extend the width of my body. No tank top fully covers my breasts and let's not talk about my derriere!"

Thad just held her. Her head was pressed against his chest. He rested his chin on the top of her head. He wished she could see what he saw. Unfortunately, this world had her seeing herself through its lens.

"Babe, I don't know how to express to you in words how beautiful you are to me. I love every curve of your body. Your stomach, your breasts, your hips and your derriere. I don't want you to lose a thing. After we get married, I certainly don't want you hiding it from me either. I believe in the marriage bed, kitchen, stairs, living room, back porch, every room of the house being undefiled. I love the way you look, smell and feel. I just want you to love it too. I wouldn't have approached you if I wasn't attracted to you."

Zoe kept her head on his chest, but he backed away when he felt moisture on his chest and heard her sniffle.

"Zoe, babe, are you ok?"

"Yes. I'm ok."

"Alright, prove it."

"How?" She asked, wiping away her tears.

"Are you wearing that tank top underneath this shirt?"

"Yes," she answered reluctantly.

"Ok. Take off the t-shirt and let me see you in your tank top."

"What? No! You're running out Thad!" She was laughing and backing away.

"I'm serious. Take it off."

"Ok. Fine. If this will make you leave me alone about it." She pulled the t-shirt over her head, readjusted her tank top and took her head scarf off too.

"Are you happy now?"

"Not quite. Come here and give me another hug."

She embraced him again.

"Zoe, are you really ok?"

"Yes, why?"

"Because you're still sniffling."

"That's because I'm trying to get over the fact that your armpits smell like a dead possum!"

"What?" he laughed and stepped away. "Oh! you've got jokes! I'm over here trying to console you and you've got stinky jokes. Ok. I see how you are."

Zoe was bent over in laughter. "I'm sorry baby but you need a shower." She continued to laugh at him pretending to be hurt by her words.

He sniffed his underarm and frowned a little. Zoe really went into a fit of laughter at that point.

"So, you think this is funny?"

She was laughing so hard that she couldn't talk. She only shook her head to say no. Before she knew it, Thad was over her with his armpit in her face telling her to sniff again. She laughed even harder. Thad pulled her in for a kiss, in the midst of her laughter.

"Alright, babe. I'm going home to get this funk off of me. I'll call you later, ok?"

"Ok."

He grabbed his keys and swatted her on the butt on his way out of the door.

She jumped in surprise but relished in how she felt with him. She watched him back out of the driveway before locking and closing the door.

"God, I love this man!"

Chapter 15

Thanksgiving Changed Everything...

Thanksgiving Day was a dream for Zoe. This would be her first time having a man over for the holidays with her family. She prepared most of the items on the menu. She cooked baked turkey, collards with white rice, macaroni and cheese, string bean casserole, baked ham, sweet potato pie, cherry pie and of course cranberry sauce adorned the table. She also made her famous seafood salad. Christmas decorations were everywhere. The scent of apple cinnamon candles and food filled the house. It was chilly in Summerville, so she lit the fireplace. Dinner started at four o'clock and it got dark shortly after five o'clock. This was just in time to turn on the lights that decorated her yard. She was proud to brag to Tyler that Thad put them up for her.

Thad arrived at her home around three o'clock. He admired everything about the house. He loved how it smelled, how clean and organized it was and that it was this way all the time. He watched her as she touched up last minute items while refusing his help on anything. She made him a sprite with cranberry drink, gave him the remote and told him to keep Mr. Hundley company.

Mr. Hundley had on a holiday shirt with a bell on it. Therefore, whenever he moved, his bell rung. It was supposed to help Zoe keep up with him when the crowd arrived. Everyone loved Mr. Hundley, so she didn't want to crate him. He hung out by the fireplace on his dog bed instead.

Zoe noticed Thad watching her, but she was too busy to care. She wanted everything to be perfect for her guest. She went into the dining room and turned on Christmas jazz music. She was ready.

At four o'clock, Thad's daughters were ringing her doorbell. She propped it open so that everyone would be able to just come in. They greeted each other with hugs. Autumn made it a point to hug her a little longer. It was a sincere hug.

Ava and Autumn fell in love with Zoe's house. They complimented her on everything. Mr. Hundley stole their hearts. Autumn ended up carrying Mr. Hundley everywhere with her. He wouldn't leave her side. Thad stood back and took it all in.

Her parents arrived and Thad immediately went outside to greet them. He helped her parents in and brought the dishes in that her Mom made. His relationship with her parents was growing and going smoothly. Thad made it a point to visit her church on the Sundays that his Elders preached. He arrived to church late but just in time for praise and worship and the sermon.

He and Pastor Reed seemed to really hit it off. They spent time in Pastor's Reed office talking about the word of God and certainly about Zoe. He even assisted Pastor Reed in service by taking part in the program with reading scriptures, doing the prayer, or presiding over the service.

Zoe was in awe of how fast everything was happening and how strategic God was and is in putting things together for her and Thad. Zoe's mom joined her and Thad's daughters in the kitchen. Tyler and her family came by as well. Zoe's other siblings were there with their spouses and children. She was the only one who wasn't married or didn't have children. She was the oldest and this made her dread the holidays. However, this year was different because of Thad being a part of her life.

Dinner went smoothly. They all ate in the dining room. Zoe's brothers wanted to watch the game, so they ventured into the living room shortly after. Zoe peaked outside and noticed that it was dark.

"Alright everyone! It's our tradition that we turn on the Christmas lights on Thanksgiving night. So, I need everyone to gather around please. Put on your coats because it's a bit chilly outside and let's light it up!"

All of the children ran outside. Some had on coats and others didn't. Zoe's parents took one of her throw blankets out of the basket in the living room and shared it on the outside. Once everyone was outside, Zoe opened the blinds to her living room and turned on the tree lights. She heard her family and friends cheering. Thad stood on the outside along with them, but, wasn't smiling at all. He was just staring at her. She couldn't make out his facial expression. She felt nervous and hoped she hadn't upset him in some way or another.

She fastened her coat and headed outside as well. She turned on the outside lights and everyone was cheering once again. They all cheered, except Thad. She quieted everyone and publicly thanked Thad for his assistance with the outside decorations. She joked about not having to climb a ladder this year to hang lights. Everyone commented on what a great job he did. He still said nothing. He had no reaction. Zoe walked over to Thad and lightly touched his wrist. She hesitantly looked up at him as he solemnly looked down at her.

"Thad, are you ok?"

"Yes. I'm ok. Would you mind if I addressed your family and friends?"

"Sure. I think," She still couldn't understand why he was behaving the way he was. What she didn't know was Thad couldn't react because the voice of the Lord was louder to him than the people surrounding him. He was in the presence of God. He stepped out of Zoe's grasp and turned to her family and friends.

"Excuse me everyone, I'd like to say something please."

The parents hushed their children as Thad proceeded to speak.

"Did you all enjoy dinner?"

"Yes, everything was delicious," some cheered.

"Everything was beautiful," others added.

"What about the lights? Did you all really enjoy the lights?"

"Yes, they're really pretty!" Zoe's seven-year-old niece offered with a hint of a giggle.

"I'm glad that you all enjoyed everything. The reason that I'm speaking to you all tonight at one time is because I have something important to say and I need every one of you present when I say it."

Thad turned to Zoe, grabbed her hand, looked her in the eyes and the only thing that could be heard were gasps. Zoe felt like she'd stopped breathing for a moment.

"Zoe, the past four months with you have been simply incredible. Had someone told me in June that I'd meet someone as fabulous as you in July, I wouldn't have believed them. Nevertheless, I have no doubt in my mind that you are the woman the Lord has set aside for me. I love you and I want to spend the rest of my life with you. I've already met with your Father and asked his permission to do this. I've also consulted with my daughters. They have all agreed. So, now I'm asking you, Zoe Acacia Reed," he knelt down on one knee. "Would you do me the honor of being my wife?"

He opened the box revealing a beautiful ring and Zoe felt like she was going pass out. She glanced at her parents and they were both smiling. She glanced at Ava and Autumn and they both gave her a thumbs up simultaneously.

"Yes! Yes Thad, I'll marry you!"

He gave her a quick peck on the lips and whispered in her ear. "You'll get the real kiss later."

Her family and friends all ran to them to hug them and congratulate them. Zoe could barely see straight because her eyes were flooded with tears. Thad's were too. They all congregated back into the house. The adults and the little girls all admired her ring. Two carats in white gold were more than she could ask for. It was the perfect fit.

The guys constantly shook his hand or patted Thad on the back. They all hung out in the living room, while the children played upstairs in the loft on the Xbox. The women all seemed to gather in the kitchen where they pulled out more pies and cakes with whipped cream.

Thad was brave enough to come into the kitchen with Zoe. He embraced her from behind and kissed the top of her forehead. Zoe's eyes stretched because of the level of affection he was displaying and because of what she felt behind her when he embraced her. The women giggled like schoolgirls and mumbled under their breath. This was the first time Thad and Zoe showed this type of affection in the front of them.

"Alright you two, get a room!" Tyler interjected. The ladies laughed a little harder.

"As soon as you all leave, we just might!" Thad quipped.

The ladies erupted in laughter then and Thad released Zoe but not before placing a kiss right below her earlobe and playfully swatting her on her butt. Zoe just shook her head as she blushed. She was glad that she was behind the island because she was sure that she felt her knees buckle a little when he kissed her.

Her guests took the hint and slowly left after giving each other hugs goodbye. Congratulations filled the room once more and then they were left alone. Zoe and Thad stood on the porch waving as their guests left. When the last car left her home, Thad had his arm draped over her shoulder and she hugged his waist. She looked up at him and he immediately kissed her lips. They didn't say anything to each other, they simply went back inside and closed the door. Zoe proceeded to the kitchen and just shook her head at the mess that was left behind. Dishes were in the sink and the trash was overflowing. Leftover soda cans were all over the island and kitchen table. Pies were half eaten and left to be discarded. Her feet were throbbing, and her back was hurting, but she was still smiling. She was engaged! She was getting married! It was finally happening. She was not expecting this tonight, but God loves surprising his children.

"How long are you going to stand there daydreaming, Mrs. Wescott?" Thad pulled Zoe out of her thoughts with the sound of his voice.

"I'm not Mrs. Wescott yet, Sir!"

"Well, you will be soon enough," he embraced her from the front this time.

"How soon are you talking, Sir?"

"I can't wait that long, Zoe. It's November now so let's aim for April or May. That would give us five to six months to work with."

Zoe backed away in shock. "What? Did you just say five to six months? Thad, I have to find a dress, a decorator, a photographer, a venue, and a caterer!"

Thad pulled her back into the embrace and stopped her from talking by kissing her very passionately. He lightly nipped and sucked on her bottom lip.

"Thad I —."

He kissed her again.

"Thad I'm serious."

Another kiss.

"Thad come on we have to talk —."

He kissed her once more.

" — about this."

"There is nothing to talk about, Zoe. We will go to the bank tomorrow and I will add you onto my personal account. Whatever it costs, I will cover it. You know a lot of people so I'm sure you can make it happen if money isn't an issue, right?"

"Yes, I suppose," she said as Thad lightly rocked her body from side to side as if they were dancing to music in their heads.

"What about colors and a theme for the wedding? Do we want it outside or inside? What about a DJ?"

Thad released Zoe from the embrace, took her hands, twisted the diamond on her finger and looked her in the eyes. "Zoe, I honestly could marry you in the bathroom while standing in the front of a toilet. I could care less. I just want you to be my wife. Why don't you incorporate Tyler and your mom with the details? Run them by me so I'm in the loop and let me know how much everything will cost. But baby, I can't go much longer with not being able to touch you, make love to you, have you all to myself. If I knew that you didn't have to have a wedding, I'd say let's fly to Vegas tomorrow and get married. However, I know that you want, and you deserve more than that. Let me know how I can help but I want this to happen as soon as possible. Are you ok with that? I don't want to move faster than you'd like."

Zoe sighed in surrender. "Ok! We can get married in April or May, but we need to set a specific date. Vendors can't book me based on an approximation."

"Alright, let's get a calendar."

They decided on April 14th. Zoe was nervous, ecstatic, and overwhelmed with joy. Her life was rapidly changing, and she was enjoying every moment.

"Ok, Mrs. soon-to-be Wescott, let's clean up this kitchen."

"Sounds like a plan, Mr. Wescott!"

They worked together and cleaned the kitchen, bathroom and living area. They moved without any direction. He knew what was next without being told. It was as if they'd been together for years. Zoe smiled as she watched him move around her house with Mr. Hundley on his heel.

The house was finally cleaned with the leftovers put away. They settled on the couch and Zoe pulled the calendar out again. She found a clean sheet of paper and they discussed the wedding plans. Within two hours, the main details were covered. They decided on coral, gold and white as the wedding colors. The theme would be diamonds and pearls with birdcages. They decided to have artificial white birds within the cages on each table. They concluded to have the wedding at his church because it was larger than hers and because his church had a reception hall. One of her clients decorates so she'd ask her to do the honors. Her cousin owns a catering business and does all the catering for the church. She'd book her. Her photographer for the salon also does weddings so she texted him while they were planning and booked him. Thad's sound-man for the church is also a disc jockey. Thad would book him.

They decided to have a small wedding party. Between her siblings, in-laws, nieces and nephews, she couldn't have anyone else on her side, other than Tyler. His daughters, of course, would stand as bridesmaids as well. The groomsmen consisted of the Prophet who spoke into their lives, Jamal his armor bearer, and her brothers.

"See, I told you that everything we need is already right in the front of us," he wrapped his arm around her, as they sat on the couch, and rubbed her arm in reassurance.

"I know. This is just all happening so fast. I mean, one day I'm in the car having a fit because it seemed as if God turned a deaf ear to me. Four months later, I'm planning my wedding. It's like he sped my life up!"

"Well, baby, that's how God works. Just when it seems like he's forgotten about us, he literally puts what we've been praying for right in our laps. Speaking of laps, why don't you come on over a little bit."

Zoe laughed and playfully popped him on his knee before standing and helping him up.

"Why are you pulling me up?"

"Because whenever you start that 'fresh talk', that's my cue to tell you to go home so we can stay saved!"

He wrapped his arms around her thick waist, and she sighed against him. *He smells so good*, she thought to herself.

"Alright, I'll go. He let her go, picked up his jacket and put it on, "Can I have a kiss first though?"

Zoe reached up, wrapped her arms around his neck, as she stood on her tiptoe, and gave him a long, lingering kiss that caused him to whisper Jesus' name.

"My Lord, please let April 14th hurry up and get here! I don't think I can take much more," he said as he pressed his forehead against the top of her head.

She laughed at his comment and pushed him towards the door.

"Here's your to-go box and Goodnight, Mr. Wescott. Call me when you get home, ok?"

"Ok. I love you."

"I love you, too."

Chapter 16
CALL 911- NOW!

Good news as wells as bad news travels fast. The news of the engagement was good to some and bad to others. It was gut wrenching for Sis. Yolanda and a few other women who had their fingers crossed cried secret tears too. Thad was truly a desired man! All of the members weren't there because of the word. Some of them just liked who was bringing the word. They loved watching his muscles under his vest. They loved seeing him in his tailored suits and fresh haircut. His cologne sent many of the women into a frenzy, old and young. Many tried to get close to him by requesting "counseling sessions" during the week, but Thad was a wise man. He always had a member of his ministerial staff within the office along with them. Those sessions didn't last long and slowly became less frequent once the word spread that women would not be found alone with him.

Zoe's church was packed on Sunday. Her father made the announcement of the engagement prior to his sermon. Thad was right there with Zoe on the front row and they danced together as most of the congregation danced with them. Just as Thad had some secret and not so secret admirers, so did Zoe. She had a few guys at the church who were watching her but never found the courage to approach her. They were on age with her Father and feared him with a vengeance. Some were significantly younger than her and feared her brothers. However, she was with who God wanted her to be with. She'd prayed years ago against any counterfeits of a husband. She expected to not have to deal with random men because of the prayer but she was not prepared to feel unattractive or invisible in the process.

When a prayer like that is prayed, it's like God puts a shield around you. Men will see you and like you, but they won't be able to get close to you if they are not the one. Zoe had to be reminded that a delayed blessing was for her protection. God had someone better for her. When Zoe's service was over. They greeted everyone and received lots of compliments on the ring and congratulations. Some were genuine, and some were not. Nevertheless, they could care less. God was amidst them. Thad followed Zoe home and she dropped her car off. They then headed over to Thad's church and walked in together. The church went into a praise as soon as they walked through the door. The presiding Elder ushered the people into a deeper realm of praise as they rejoiced because of the engagement of this couple.

Sis. Yolanda wanted to spit fire. She sat in her normal seat in a bright yellow suit with black trimming. She wore a yellow hat with a black rim. Her lips were lined with black liner and lip gloss. She looked like a huge banana that frowned. Someone should really tell her that lining your lips in black with clear lip gloss was no longer being done.

Thad took his seat on the pulpit, but Zoe sat on the front row. Ava and Autumn sat directly behind Zoe. They almost felt as if they had to protect her in some way. He graced the congregation with the official announcement of their engagement and let them know that the members of the congregation were invited. Zoe's father did the same at her church as well.

Thad preached a heartfelt message on having love in their hearts and not carrying ugly things in their hearts that are mentioned in Galatians 5:19-21 of the bible. The sounds of "amen" and "help me Lord" filled the church. Fans waved, hats moved, tears flowed, and hearts were changed. However, Sis. Yolanda's heart only hardened. Her heart grew darker by the second. She couldn't understand how Zoe was still alive and well after she planted those seeds in her yard. The guy in Savannah guaranteed her that it would work. She'd have to try something else.

When the benediction was said, many of the women embraced Zoe to see and compliment her on the ring. Several said congratulations and some looked at the ring, rolled their eyes then walked away. Others didn't greet her at all.

Sis. Yolanda, however, had to see this ring and make her next move. She sashayed her way over to Zoe. Ava and Autumn stood next to Zoe as well. Ava and Sis. Yolanda always had a friendship, but Ava also knew that she wanted Thad. Ava greeted her but her stance said, *don't try nothing stupid.*

Sis. Yolanda ignored the look Ava gave her and made her way to Zoe. "Hi Zoe, let me see that ring, girl!"

Zoe reluctantly held out her hand to Sis. Yolanda. Thad noticed the interaction and just about ran from the pulpit to defend his upcoming bride.

"Sis. Yolanda, what are you doing?"

"Oh, nothing Pastor. I'm just admiring this beautiful ring." she lightly touched Zoe's hand and when she pulled away Zoe noticed a blue stain on the ring but thought nothing of it. She was surrounded with people, so anyone could've done it. Sis. Yolanda walked away with a satisfied grin on her face. Thad and his daughters noticed it, but Zoe was still talking with the other ladies.

They left the church and Thad, Zoe and his daughters decided to go back to his house for dinner. On the drive over, Thad heard Zoe moan a little and asked if she was ok. She confirmed that she was. When they arrived at Thad's house. He went to her door to help her out of the car. As she stood, she fell backwards, but Thad caught her.

"Zoe, are you ok? Zoe!"

Zoe had lost consciousness. Ava and Autumn pulled into the yard at that very moment and saw Thad holding Zoe. They left the car on and ran towards them.

"Dad, what's wrong? Zoe!" They frantically yelled. "Dad what's wrong with her?"

"I don't know. Call 911."

The ambulance arrived faster than they had anticipated. Thad still had Zoe in his arms. He was afraid to move her. He just prayed as Ava called 911. Autumn stood next to him and prayed as well.

They got her into the ambulance as quick as possible. Autumn found Zoe's purse and called her parents to tell them what was happening. The ambulance rushed her to the hospital in downtown Charleston. Her family rushed their as well. Her mom called Tyler and she came too.

When they arrived at the hospital, Zoe was unresponsive. Her family and friends all waited in the waiting room and prayed. As the Dr. checked her pulse and vitals repeatedly, they noticed the light blue film on her left hand near the ring. Her blood pressure and heart rate were extremely low. The nurse ran out of the room and asked Thad about it. He came in and saw the blue on her hands as well. Immediately, the Lord spoke to him and said, "witchcraft." He let the nurse know that he didn't know what it was, but he had an idea of who it came from.

"Just please do everything that you can to revive her," he felt tears swell in his eyes. He went into the waiting area and Zoe's Dad noticed that Thad was very upset.

"What's wrong, Thad?" he asked

"It's witchcraft y'all. The Lord said witchcraft."

"You know what, Yolanda did bring her fat behind over there and touched Zoe," Autumn chimed in.

"Oh my God! Y'all we have to pray. Yolanda has shared stories with me over the years of how her family has taken people out with witchcraft. She goes to some man in another state to get her stuff," Ava added.

"Ok. We're going to pray, because my bible tells me that no weapon that is formed against us shall prosper," Zoe's Mom added through teary eyes but a confident heart.

They held hands and Zoe's Mom prayed a prayer of faith. While they were praying, a few strangers and nurses chimed in to agree with the prayers. The sound filled the floor of the hospital. People who hadn't walked in years started moving their legs at the sound of the prayer. People who hadn't spoken in months began to say, "thank ya Lord!" Miracles were happening in their midst that they had no clue about.

While they were still praying. The doctor ran into the hall and screamed into the waiting room that they were in.

"She's awake!" He ran back into her room.

Zoe was crying and speaking in tongues. Thad and her parents ran to her bed. Her siblings, Tyler and Thad's daughters stood in the room but out of the way. The doctor checked her vitals again and everything was normal. Zoe looked around the room as she tried to focus her eyes. She was barely audible but still speaking in tongues.

Her mom heard her say, "No weapon that is formed against me shall prosper. Satan will not win. Because God is for me, who can be against me."

"Yes baby, that's it. You speak the word," her Mom hollered out in a praise.

Thad had his hand on her shoulder and was inwardly praying along with her.

"How are you feeling, baby girl," her dad asked?

"Dad, it was witchcraft," Zoe's eyes were closed as tears rolled down her face. She cleared her throat. "When I was out, the Lord took me in the spirit and replayed everything to me. It was Yolanda. She touched my ring and placed something on me. But God is mighty, and he is sovereign. He promised me in Psalms 91 that, 'nothing shall by any means harm me'."

The nurse came rushing back in. She had a test report in her hand. They were able to retrieve some of the substance from Zoe's hand and test it.

The nurse spoke, "It was an herb of some sort. It was poisonous and so potent that by simply touching it you could die."

"Yolanda was wearing a yellow glove," Ava offered.

"That witch! I'm going to have to put a stop to this! Nurse is it possible to get this report to the police and press charges?" Thad quizzed.

"Yes, and if this woman is as dangerous as you say she is, the police may be the only ones who can stop her," the nurse added.

"I'll be right back," Thad stepped into the hall and called his friend on the police force. Within thirty minutes he was there with a detective. Once again, news travels fast so some of the church members of both churches came to the hospital as well. So did Yolanda but she remained away from everyone. She changed into a different wig, a black sweater and jeans. No one even noticed she was there.

The detective took the report from the nurse and called the captain of the police department. They faxed over a warrant to search Yolanda's property to the hospital's fax machine.

Yolanda saw some of Zoe's family members leaving the room and they looked sad. They were actually happy about Zoe being awake and alive but sad about Yolanda being so evil! She misinterpreted their facial expressions. She felt a sense of boldness when Thad stepped out of the room and made her way over to him.

"You actually have the nerve to be here? What is wrong with you woman? I don't want you. I've never wanted you! I don't find you attractive. I don't think about you in a positive way. I find you atrocious to be honest with you! Why are you here Yolanda?" He screamed in her face and forced her back against the wall as he stepped towards her.

Some of the church members, Zoe's family and friends, along with the nurses had to pull him back from her. He wasn't going to hurt her physically, but he wanted to get his point across in a clear and firm way. He didn't expect to come off on her the way he did, but he had enough. He'd already lost one wife to death. He would not lose another!

"Calm down, Thad. Let's walk man," Zoe's brother offered.

Yolanda stood there embarrassed, angered and afraid. She'd never seen Thad like that. Her feelings were so hurt. She felt low, but she wasn't sorry for what she'd done to Zoe. Just then the detective and police officer emerged from the reception area with the fax in hand.

They called her name and she looked up with fear in her eyes. They let her know that they have a warrant to search her property. Initially, she refused but when she saw all of the eyes of the people who disliked her looking at her, she digressed.

They put on gloves and started looking through her purse. They didn't have to go any further. They dumped the contents of her purse on a huge plastic cover and laid it on an empty nearby desk. Everything that they needed was there. They found a Ziploc bag that had a medicine bottle in it with a thick blue substance. She also had the pair of yellow gloves in another Ziploc bag. She was so stupid; she even had the instructions on how to use the substance to kill someone without being caught. They confiscated the substances and took it to be tested in the hospital lab. She was instructed not to leave the premises. The hospital's security guard took her to his office until the testing was done. It was on the same floor as Zoe's room.

The test results matched. They identified the substance. They went to the security guard's office and Yolanda looked as if she could poop in her clothes when she saw the handcuffs.

"Yolanda Greenlocke?"

"Y-yes."

"You are under arrest for the attempted murder of Zoe Reed!" He placed her hands behind her back and slipped on the handcuffs as tight as he could.

"Ouch! That hurts!"

"That was my goal," the officer smirked.

"What do you mean attempted murder?" Yolanda asked.

"You tried to kill Zoe Reed, but it didn't work," the detective answered.

Yolanda didn't even try to hide the look of disappointment on her face. She looked like a walking devil. They walked her out of the room and towards the exit. Unfortunately for Yolanda, they had to pass the area where Zoe's family and friends were at. All of the church people who were there would see her in handcuffs. She held her head down in defeat.

Zoe's Mom heard all of the commotion and stepped in the hall to see what was going on. Zoe was alert and fussing about going home. She was concerned about Thad and asked her Mom to open the door so she could hear. Her mom did. Just then, the nurse came running towards the people in the hall for Zoe. Zoe's Mom leaned on the wall by Zoe's room door to protect her. Her oldest son came and stood next to her to protect her and Zoe.

"Detective, wait!"

"What is it," the detective asked?

The crowd was speaking negatively and loudly about Yolanda. They didn't care if she could hear them. They all disliked her.

"We kept a file of other women who died with a blue substance that we could not identify until today. We ran some tests and they all match the substance from Ms. Greenlocke's purse," the nurse explained.

The officer held Yolanda in place as she began to struggle. She sobbed relentlessly and said, "I just wanted to be loved. Every time I tried to get close to a man, some hussy came along and took him away from me. My Daddy never loved me, cause some lady took him from my mama. Why did he have to leave me though?" Tears sprang from her eyes. "My high school boyfriend was stolen from me by my best friend. My college boyfriend, well I tried to make him my boyfriend, but he said I wasn't his type. His girlfriend flaunted their relationship in my face. She had to die. She just had to!"

"How long have you been using this substance against people, Yolanda," Thad questioned?

The waiting room grew quiet as everyone sat in disbelief waiting for her to speak. They knew she was evil and couldn't be trusted, but none of them knew to what extent until now.

"I came across it at the age of seven."

"Where did you get it from at seven years old Yolanda?" Thad asked in shock.

"My mother picked it up from a man in Georgia. She taught me how to use it. She took me to the lady who stole my Father and I put it on her. She died within hours, but my Daddy never came back. Why didn't he come back for me, Thad?" Her sobs got louder and louder.

She walked up to Thad with the officer still holding her wrists. His daughters stood in the front of her. "I'm sorry about Zoe and about your first wife. I just wanted you to love me, Thad. That's all I wanted."

Thad stepped in the front of his daughters to face Yolanda. His fist were balled up at his sides. The girls both dropped their purse simultaneously.

"What are you talking about 'regarding my first wife', Yolanda?

"Oh my," the nurse interrupted!

"What is it," the detective asked?

"I'm just looking over the names of the people. There's a total of eleven women here who's cause of death was not found. The blue substance was involved."

"What are the names of the victims," asked the detective?

"Please tell me you don't have Mary Wescott on that list! Please tell you don't!" Thad chimed in and tried to get to Yolanda.

The nurse slowly lifted her face from the list and said, "Mary Wescott was the fourth person reported with the blue substance."

Thad, Ava and Autumn abruptly turned to look at Yolanda.

"You killed my wife? You killed my wife!" Thad yelled.

It went from being a question to a shocking confirmation. Thad reached for Yolanda and grabbed her neck to strangle her. Zoe's dad and the other men rushed over and pulled him away. However, Ava and Autumn stepped in just in time and began punching her wherever their hands could land. Screams filled the hospital. The ladies and a few men pulled Thad's daughters off of Yolanda. They were crying and looked as if they wanted to kill her.

"You killed my mother!" Ava retorted. "You tried to get close to me to be a mother figure when you killed my mother? How did you do it?" She yelled, "Answer me!"

Yolanda breathed slowly and lifted her head. "I greeted her after church and touched her, then her belly. I'm so sorry, Ava. I really did enjoy our friendship."

WHAP!

That was the only sound you could hear other than the monitors in the hall. Ava slapped Yolanda so hard that blood spilled from her nose and her mouth.

"Alright, that's enough. We're taking her to the county for processing," the detective interjected.

Yolanda was taken to the police station. After all of the evidence was turned in, she was processed and held without a bond. She killed a total of eleven women since she was age seven. She would be sentenced to life in prison without parole.

Chapter 17

The Day We've Waited For...

Zoe recovered quickly. Thad's daughters returned home. However, Thad kept a close eye on Zoe and became very protective of her.

Zoe returned to the salon because sitting in the house all day was driving her nuts.

Tyler was put on assignment by Thad to keep an eye on her and make sure she didn't over exert herself. The wedding plans resumed, and things were progressing along smoothly.

Thad sent a letter to the prison removing Yolanda from their membership at the church. An announcement was made at the church regarding her arrest and why. This seemed to cause a tsunami of people to come and join the church.

Thad's birthday was on December 21st. They had a small gathering at B & R Seafood on Shem Creek. Thad's focus was the wedding and therefore a birthday party could wait until next year. Her parents were once again reminded of his age in comparison to hers. However, the love in their eyes for each other caused them to overlook that fact.

Christmas, New Years and Valentine's Day came and went. Thad and Zoe, along with their friends and family, celebrated together and got along well. The wedding day quickly approached. April 14th seemed to have creeped up on them.

Zoe awoke the morning of her wedding and looked around her hotel suite at the Charleston Place Hotel. They decided to make her house a rental and she'd move in with Thad. She moved everything out and took with her what she would need for the week. They combined and got rid of furniture from both places. Thad's house now felt like her house. She was reluctant at first but then she learned that no other woman has ever occupied his home except his daughters. When his first wife died, he sold that house and moved into this current house. She'd taken Mr. Hundley over to Thad's house on yesterday and got him settled in. She missed him barking first thing in the morning and greeting her with a wet kiss on her hand. She'd see him in a few hours though.

Her week long stay at the hotel had been remarkable. In the mornings, she awoke to shrimp and grits with cold orange juice and at night, she ate lobster and ribeye steaks.

Thad came over every day to check on her and reminded her of what would happen on the night of April 14th. The closer it got to the date, the more they wanted each other.

In a few hours, however, the wait would be over. Her dress hung in the hotel's closet. She laid her head on the pillow next to her and admired her ring. The past nine months were amazing. God proved himself to her in a major way! Yolanda tried but even she couldn't ruin God's plan for her life.

Room service knocked on the door and pulled her away from her thoughts. She wrapped her long, white, silk robe around her curves and headed to the door. Her breakfast was brought in followed by her Mom, Sister, Tyler and Thad's daughters. Thad had a limo bring them to the hotel, so they could change there. Zoe briefly greeted them and ran into the bathroom to brush her teeth and freshen up. They all ate breakfast and reminisced on how far the Lord had brought her. She cried, her mom cried, and the others did too.

Breakfast ended, and room service was called to come and clean up their mess. Zoe showered and prepared to have her hair and makeup done by Tyler. Tyler did all of the lady's hair on Friday. She only had to add a few finishing touches and do their makeup. Zoe's makeup and hair were done last. The ladies looked so beautiful in their gold dresses with coral trim and coral colored belt. Zoe began to cry again.

"Alright now, don't be messing up my hard work with those tears! You better suck it up! Stop all that dog-gone crying," Tyler fussed.

The other ladies laughed at Zoe being reprimanded.

Zoe pulled herself together. Finally, it was time to put on her dress. Her mom, sister, and Tyler helped her. She looked absolutely gorgeous. It was designed with a beaded lace appliqué covering the cap sleeve. It was a V-neck trumpet gown with sparkles. The skirt was made of mesh godets for easy movements. It was finalized with a coral, diamond belt across her waist and a chapel train that was floor length. The train had a lace and diamond trim. She wore her natural hair in a pulled back afro ponytail. She graced her ears with diamond earrings with a pearl. Her necklace matched it. She dripped a scented oil, that she knew would drive Thad crazy, in her hair, behind her ears and on her wrists. Her feet were covered in a pair of coral sling backs by Salvatore Ferragamo.

She made sure Tyler had Thad's ring, her bouquet and gifts for her parents and Thad's daughters. His parents were no longer alive, and he was the only child. They left the room and proceeded to the wedding. When they arrived, the parking lot was packed. Cars were aligned on the side of the road. The church sign read Congrats Pastor Thad and Zoe Wescott. Zoe blushed as butterflies settled in her stomach.

Zoe noticed that Thad's car wasn't at the church. Her heart dropped into the pit of her stomach. They were fifteen minutes early, but Thad was never late! Thirty minutes went by and Zoe started to panic. They were now fifteen minutes late for their wedding. This was not like Thad at all! Autumn called his cell phone over and over again, but it went straight to voicemail. Zoe called her brothers, but they hadn't seen or heard from him. They were at the church and waiting as well. Everyone was there except Thad.

"I knew this was too good to be true," Zoe said as she twisted her ring back and forth on her hand. The ladies' voices filled the limo when Zoe said that.

"No, that's not true. Thad is coming. He's just running late!" one said, and the others agreed.

Zoe felt tears streaming down her face.

"No, no, no, no! You will not mess up my hard work ma'am," Tyler said as she moved from her seat and squeezed in next to Zoe. She wiped Zoe's eyes with some Kleenex from her bra.

Zoe frowned and the ladies all laughed at Zoe fighting not to have Tyler's breast stained tissue on her cheekbones. While they were laughing Thad's, car pulled up. He ran over to the limo and Zoe tried to open the door.

"No! He can't see you yet!" Zoe's mom yelled while Tyler held her hands from opening the door.

Thad leaned into the driver seat and yelled pass the driver. "Zoe, can you hear me?"

"Yes, what's going on? Why are you so late, Thad?" She started to cry again.

"I'm sorry, baby. You'll understand why in a few but it's going to make you happy. Just trust me ok?"

Zoe looked confused and so did the other ladies, but Tyler didn't. She was grinning from ear to ear.

Zoe gave Tyler a look that said, *if you know something you better tell me or I'm going to kill you.*

Tyler gripped Zoe's face. "Look at me and don't turn around until I tell you to."

Just then Zoe heard the ladies squealing with excitement. Zoe tried to turn around to see what was happening, but Tyler had a death grip on her. After a minute or so, she released her grip. The wedding director came outside and escorted the ladies from the limo. Zoe's Mom gave her a hug and a kiss before exiting the vehicle.

Tyler and Zoe sat there holding hands in anticipation of going into the church. Zoe noticed that Tyler's eyes were glossy.

"Uh-uh, nope, don't you do that, Tyler!"

"I can't help it. My friend is getting married," she whined as tears fell! Zoe held her head back and fanned back tears.

The director returned to the limo, flung the door open and said, "It's your time lady!"

Tyler reached into her bra and pulled out more tissue. They both fell into a fit of laughter without having to say a word. They stepped out of the vehicle and Tyler helped Zoe up the steps and into the church.

"Ready?" she asked.

"Ready," Zoe replied.

"Ok," Tyler kissed Zoe on the cheek and reached into the box next to her. Come on Laylah! Laylah, Tyler's daughter came around the corner with Mr. Hundley in a tuxedo with bells and the ring on his back. He tried to jump on Zoe to say hello, but Laylah kept pulling him into the sanctuary, so his bell could ring.

Zoe's laughter was drowned out by the surprise and ooh's and ah's of the people. At that moment, she heard the beginning of the song, "All of Me" by John Legend. It was *their* song.

Her dad appeared in the vestibule. He was in his clergy robe, but he was there to walk her down the aisle.

"You look absolutely beautiful," he whispered in her ear as he hugged her.

"Thanks, Daddy."

"Ready?" he asked.

A tear fell uncontrollably from her eye. "Yes Sir."

The doors of the church opened, and the words of the song filled the place. Everyone was standing and watching her. She was watching him. Her dad walked her half of the way and her Mom joined them. She kissed her Mom on the cheek and tears spilled from both of their eyes.

When she reached Thad, he was a bucket of tears. His groomsmen gave up on trying to pass him a handkerchief. The tears were coming faster than he could wipe them.

The Bishop's voice sounded off in the microphone attached to his clergy robe. "Who giveth this woman to this man?"

"We do!" her parents said in unison.

Zoe's dad walked her mom to her seat and then he joined the Bishop to assist with the wedding ceremony. Zoe and Thad finally stopped crying and the ceremony continued.

When it was time to kiss the bride, Thad lifted Zoe's veil, and stared at her for a moment. Zoe began to feel uncomfortable. Then she noticed a tear. He leaned in and kissed her as if no one was in the room. He took his time. He kissed her slow and easy. She stood there and let him. He was her husband after all, and she was his wife.

Chapter 18

Chocolate Vs Steel

*** (DISCLAIMER) If you are not married, I don't suggest continuing any further.
If you are married, after reading this, go and have a blast with your husband or wife!

Cheers filled the room as Thad and Zoe greeted their guests and took a few pictures. When they got to the reception hall, everyone was happy and smiling. They seemed to be enjoying the h'orderves. The wedding party was announced and when they called Thad and Zoe's name, she turned into a ten-year-old. They glided onto the dance floor and danced as if no one was watching.

When the dance was over, her dad and mom came up and danced with her. They had so much fun. Zoe cried and laughed more than she could ever imagine. Thad danced with his daughters as well. The bridal party eventually joined them.

They sat and ate their dinner. Soon, it was time for the bride and groom to depart. The limo took them back to the hotel that Zoe stayed at all week. Thad's daughters dropped off his car when the reception was over and left the keys at the front desk.

When they entered the room, it was fully decorated in coral and gold artificially colored roses. Chocolate scented candles were everywhere. Tyler paid the hotel staff to decorate for them. Zoe's parents contributed as well. They didn't want to have anything to do with their daughter having sex, but they had to contribute in some way. Thad tried to pay for everything and refuse their help. However, they beat him to the punch.

They stepped into the room and were in awe at the sight and scent of the room. It was so romantic. Jazz music played softly in the background. Thad showered and came back into the room in a terry-cloth robe. Zoe showered and came out in an all-black, crotchless, fishnet stocking from head to toe. She wore long white pearls with red platform shoes. Her makeup was light, and her lips were bare.

When Thad looked up and saw her. Everything that he'd held back over the past nine months came rushing forward. He got up from the bed and went to her. She leaned against the wall with one heel against the wall. She held her pearls in her hands and in between her teeth.

"You look so sexy. I'm about to tear you up!"

Zoe didn't say a word. She leaned up off of the wall. Shoved his robe to the floor to find him in only his boxers. She pushed him onto the bed and sat on top of him. She leaned over and the coolness of the pearls grazing his chest excited him. She looked into his eyes and slid his bottom lip into her mouth and gently sucked on it.

Thad lost all sense of control and flipped her over onto the bed. Their kiss deepened. When his body landed in between her thighs and he felt those large mounds of chocolate wrap around him, he groaned as if a monster was emerging. Zoe rubbed him, kissed his bald head, nose, cheeks, and mouth. Her feet sat on the bottom of his back. When he felt them there, he realized that he had access to her most private possession.

Thad popped the pearls off of her neck and began ripping the lace stocking from her body. He scooted to get out of his boxers. She pushed and pulled with her teeth to get them down. He kicked them out of the way. His lips traveled everywhere they could reach and so did his hands.

When they became one, the pieces of the puzzle came together. His body was made for hers. Thad was more than she ever expected. His entire heart, soul and body were all hers and all that she entailed was his!

Zoe felt like silk to him, but she tasted like chocolate. His body felt like steel to her. Zoe felt her body expanding when he entered her and so did her heart. She held onto him for dear life. He grasped the top of the mattress with one hand and held her with the other. He mumbled and whispered everything that she needed to hear as he made love to her. Her eyes rolled back into her head, her toes curled, her body lifted and sunk beneath her as Thad took her to a place of the unknown. She'd been intimate before but never like this! Sex as a married woman was so different from sex as a woman who fornicates. It's especially different when you're with the person God sent to you. She was glad that the tips on her nails had some thickness to them or Thad's back would be scarred from her scratching and digging into him.

They were pretty sure that the neighbors heard them. They could care less. This older man fell in love with a sexy, curvaceous and younger woman. The road they traveled the past nine months was far from straight. It had many ups, downs, and curves too. They both just happened to be preachers looking for love. In this case, they found, an extra curvy love.

Thank you for purchasing and reading my book. Please take a moment and write a review.

More books by Melvina Carpenter:

"Single, Pregnant and Preaching"
https://www.amazon.com/dp/0692486798/ref=cm_sw_em_r_mt_dp_U__ehV6BbMFK6NGP

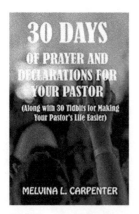

"30 Days of Prayer and Declarations of Your Pastor"
https://www.amazon.com/dp/1533265992/ref=cm_sw_em_r_mt_dp_U__oiV6BbA83K5XF

"Don't Tease the Dog"
https://www.amazon.com/dp/0692537996/ref=cm_sw_
em_r_mt_dp_U__MiV6BbWF63YTV

"Ungrateful Johnny at Christmas"
https://www.amazon.com/dp/1522823565/ref=cm_sw_
em_r_mt_dp_U__BmV6Bb0Q26NVT

"Don't Tease Me About My Hair"
https://www.amazon.com/dp/1978292031/ref=cm_sw_
em_r_mt_dp_U__hnV6BbF2M1JYX

"A Quick Guide to Publishing and Writing Your Book"

https://www.amazon.com/gp/product/1791866824/ref
=dbs_a_def_rwt_bibl_vppi_i0

All of my books are available at all major retailers online. However, please follow me at www.amazon.com/author/melvinacarpenter to be updated on future titles.

Taking Readers On a Mental Vacation

www.amazon.com/author/melvinacarpenter

To contact Melvina:
Email: melvina.carpenter@yahoo.com
Facebook: www.facebook.com/melvinacarpenterbooks
Instagram:
www.instagram.com/melvinacarpentersbooks
Twitter: www.twitter.com/mcarpentersbooks.

CPSIA information can be obtained
at www.ICGtesting.com
Printed in the USA
LVHW031129141019
634125LV00002B/778/P